WELCOME t
SPACE ZOO 1...nUL!

The Space Zoo Patrol is an elite team of animals that live and work in a massive space station above the Earth, called the Space Zoo 1. The Space Zoo Patrol is a wildly fun group that solves problems, invents cool technical gizmos, and occasionally saves the Earth by using science. NASA meets MacGyver meets the National Zoo!

The Space Zoo members represent all the continents, and are helpful and caring, but occasionally a little wacky. All of the characters, by a crazy coincidence, are named after astronauts, scientists, or Nobel Prize winners from their respective countries.

When the neighborhood kids run into a problem, and no one else can help, they turn to the Space Zoo Patrol. The Space Zoo team explores all aspects of science (astronomy, biology, chemistry, geology, math, and physics) in order to save the day.

The Space Zoo Patrol knows that science is fun and exciting, and can't wait for you to join them in their adventures in space.

Space Zoo Patrol

Think Locally…Act Galactically

Anthony Gordon Bennett

© 2016
Anthony G. Bennett

Blue Orb Books
McLean, VA 22101
www.BlueOrbWorld.com

John,
Thanks for the great edits!

Tony

Space Zoo Patrol

Space Zoo Patrol

Think Locally...Act Galactically

by Anthony Gordon Bennett

Published by Blue Orb Books
McLean, VA, USA
www.BlueOrbWorld.com

Library of Congress Control Number
2016903972

Front Cover illustration: Kaz Aizawa
Back Cover illustration: © Lifeboat Foundation (lifeboat.com)
Cover design: Ted Blair Design

Printed in the United States of America

Special thanks to:
Erik Anderson, Leslie Beck, Jack Bennett,
Michael Bennett, Tom Finn, Diana Hamblen,
John McManus,
Saylor, Jessie, and Campbell Knisely
Franklin Sherman Elementary School
The Langley School
The Potomac School

SPACE ZOO PATROL - Characters

The characters are named after scientists, astronauts, and Nobel Prize winners from their respective countries.
The charts below list the characters' names, type of animal, gender, country of origin, and their title.

SENIOR OFFICERS

Eddie   Beaver, Male, USA, Captain
         Named after Edwin "Buzz" Aldrin, US Astronaut, second man on the Moon

Jane   Owl, Female, England, Navigator
         Named after Dr. Jane Goodall, British ethologist

INTERNS

John   Penguin, Male, Antarctica, Intern
         Named after John Davis, Captain of US whaling ship, first person to set foot on Antarctica

Marcos Monkey, Male, Brazil, Intern
         Named after Marcos Pontes, Brazil's first astronaut

Lu Lu   Panda, Female, China, Intern
         Named after Dr. Lu Zhi, panda conservationist with Beijing University's Giant Panda Conservation Center

Thebe   Pygmy Hippo, Male, South Africa, Intern
         Named after Dr. Thebe Medupe, Founding Director of Astronomy Africa

Andy   Kangaroo, Male, Australia, Intern
         Named after Dr. Andy Thomas, Australian astronaut

continued

SPACE ZOO PATROL - Characters (cont.)

INTERNS (cont.)

Liz   Koala, Female, Australia, Intern
Named after Elizabeth Blackburn, Australian Nobel Prize Winner

Dave   Retriever, Male, USA, Intern

Paul   Retriever, Male, USA, Intern

JUNIOR OFFICERS

Chris   Goose, Male, Canada, Jr. Officer
Named after Chris Hadfield, Canadian Astronaut

Berty   Goose, Female, Canada, Jr. Officer
Named after Roberta Bondar, first female Canadian Astronaut

Betty   Sheep, Female, New Zealand, Jr. Officer
Named after Beatrice Tinsley, PhD Cosmology, from New Zealand

Brian   Sheep, Male, New Zealand, Jr. Officer
Named after Brian Mason, PhD Geochemistry, from New Zealand

Chi   Mandarin Duck, Female, Japanese, Jr. Officer
Named after Chiaki Mukai, first Japanese woman in space

continued

SPACE ZOO PATROL - Characters (cont.)

JUNIOR OFFICERS (cont.)
Tommy Giraffe, Male, S. Africa, Jr. Officer
> Named after Professor Thomas Odhiambo, scientist
> from Kenya

Charlize Turtle, Female, Galapagos Islands, Jr. Officer
> Named after Charles Darwin

Carlos Guinea Pig, Male, Peru, Jr. Officer
> Named after Carlos Noriega, Astronaut from Peru

Prati Orangutan, Female, Borneo, Pilot
> Named after Pratiwi Sudarmono, PhD, professor of
> molecular biology in Indonesia, and NASA payload
> specialist

NEIGHBORHOOD KIDS

Glenn	Named after John Glenn, first American astronaut to orbit Earth
Sally	Named after Sally Ride, first American female astronaut
Kali	Named after Kalpana Chawla, first woman from India in space
Mario	Named after Mario Molina, chemist, Mexican Nobel Prize winner

SPACE ZOO PATROL - Characters (cont.)

TEACHER
Miss Christa   Named after Christa McAuliffe, first teacher in space

REPORTER
Judy Laurel,   Named after Judy Resnick and Laurel Clark, both former female American astronauts

MEGA GLOBAL FOOD CORPORATION
President   Mr. Portlay
Assistant   Jim Slennar

ROBOT
Yelie   Named after Yelena Serova, first Russian woman on ISS

CHAPTER 1

The TV crew was ready to shoot a public service announcement. They had seen many officials and celebrities in the studio before, but this day was special. Dr. Walstib, was the most famous scientist on Earth. He was tall, slender, and handsome, with short white hair and a short white beard. Some speculated that George Washington Carver was a distant relative. Many in the media had tried to find out about his background but came up empty handed, except for the widely known fact that he was the youngest person to receive a PhD from MIT. He had invented the lowest cost solar panels ever made and virtually every home on Earth had several of his panels. Besides being famous, he was the world's first trillionaire. He had agreed to do the promo even though his schedule was already too busy.

The TV reporter leaned over to talk with Dr. Walstib. "All right Dr. Walstib, on the large screen behind you, which is now blank, we will have a live video feed of the exterior of your space station, and then we will have a live audio and video feed from inside the station. We'll turn to those feeds as we come to the end of the initial interview."

"Sounds good. I'm sure there won't be much to see or hear. They'll probably all be in a lab performing an experiment."

"That's fine. It will be good to see scientists hard at work. We aim for realism."

The producer looked at the reporter and counted down, "Three, two, one." Then pointed to the reporter.

"Good evening. I'm Judy Laurel. We are lucky to have with us today in the studio, the world famous Dr. Walstib. Thank you for joining us."

"Happy to be here Judy."

"Now, everyone knows about you and your solar panels, but I understand you've started a new enterprise, the Space Zoo Patrol. Tell us about them."

"We've done research all over the world with animals, and realized that many of them, such as dolphins, elephants, chimps, dogs, squirrels, wolves, crows, pigs, grey parrots, and octopi, are extremely intelligent. You've seen videos of them performing amazing feats. Or when you see a litter of say, dogs, there is one that is looking directly at you and you can tell it is trying to tell you something."

"That's how we picked our puppy," said the reporter. "My kids just knew that that pup was trying to make a connection."

"Exactly. Well, we searched throughout the world and found the animals that are the smartest, have the greatest social skills, and are physically strong, then gave them a way to communicate."

"How did you do that?" asked the reporter.

"We used the latest scanner, originally used to create a detailed 3D picture of babies in the womb, and scanned a human larynx, or voice-box. We then used a 3D printer to make a voice box out of flexible, durable, and non-allergenic plastic. We did a small operation and ten minutes later, they could talk."

"Oh my goodness," said the reporter. "That's amazing. What were their first words?"

"Many said 'Thank you.' Several said, 'Please may I have some better food?' And one said, 'Please change the channel on the TV in the lab.' "

"They sound very intelligent. What happened next?"

"They told us we were messing up the planet. They said that they had a better perspective on things than humans, and wanted to help. So I built them a space station and they've been doing scientific research ever since."

"And they are going to help us announce the beginning of the first annual Global Science Week?"

"Yes they are."

The reporter said, "I think that's our cue." The producer pushed some buttons in the studio control room, and the screen came on. Way in the distance, was a small light. Then it came into focus as the camera zoomed in on the station, painted screaming yellow and labeled 'Space Zoo 1.' Space shuttles were flying in and out of the space station.

The TV reporter smiled and said, "Take it away Dr. Walstib."

"As you see behind me, Space Zoo 1 is a state-of-the-art laboratory in space in which the Space Zoo Patrol lives and conducts experiments. The Space Zoo Patrol is a handpicked team of well-educated, well-trained scientist astronauts. They will be joining me today to say thank you to all the scientists, explorers, inventors, mathematicians, chemists, geologists, physicists, biologists, and astronomers working tirelessly to make our world a better place. Let's listen in on a typical quiet day of working in the lab."

The producer pushed a few more buttons in the control room, and the interior video and audio feed started.

It wasn't quiet, it was extremely noisy with loud rock music playing, loud talking, and loud laughing going on. The camera showed dozens of Space Zoo Patrol members, all wearing their traditional white spacesuits, dancing and laughing. Just then, someone hit a piñata. The candy, being in zero gravity, floated everywhere instead of falling to the floor. The members of the Space Zoo Patrol floated up to grab the candy pieces with their mouths.

Walstib's eyes grew wide and he motioned for the TV reporter to give him a microphone. Walstib held the microphone to his mouth and said, "Hey guys."

Everyone aboard the Space Zoo 1 heard their boss over the loudspeaker and they looked nervously at the camera that had been set up earlier. The music stopped.

Captain Eddie, a beaver from the United States, and leader of the Space Zoo Patrol, moved in front of the camera, "Hello, Dr. Walstib."

"Hi Eddie, what's happening up there?"

"We're having a little party."

"We see that."

"We're celebrating the end of our year-long study of black holes, where we found that one black hole can swallow another."

"Congratulations on the research. You guys worked hard all year. I think it's appropriate to celebrate a little bit. However, we're doing the science week promo now."

"Now?"

"Yes."

"I thought that was tomorrow."

"No, today."

Jane, an owl from England, and second in command, leaned over and whispered in Captain Eddie's ear.

Eddie looked into the camera, "I'm being told it was today."

"Thank you Jane," said Walstib.

She waved and walked back over to the rest of the Space Zoo Patrol team.

"I won't tell anyone you got that wrong," laughed Walstib.

Eddie looked a little flustered, "We try not to make any mistakes."

"Wait a minute," continued Walstib. "Didn't you hit a barn on the Oregon coastline earlier this year with a watermelon?"

"We were doing tests on space-based landing trajectories over the Pacific Ocean. Who knew a watermelon could skip over ten kilometers? Anyway, I'm sure your viewers don't need to hear that story." Eddie turned to the team behind him and lifted his arms like a conductor.

The Space Zoo Patrol members all yelled in unison, "Happy Global Science Week!"

Eddie turned back to the camera, still looking a little flustered and said, "Oh no, it looks like your camera cable is loose." He leaned into the camera, the viewers saw a close-up of Eddie's eyeball, and then the screen went blank.

The TV reporter laughed and said, "He's great!"

Walstib looked into the camera and also laughed, "Eddie may not be the best on-air personality, but he is probably the best engineer in the world."

Judy sensed an opening and said, "Dr. Walstib, why don't you tell us about any mistakes you may have made in your career."

"Oh no, it looks like your camera cable is loose too."

Walstib leaned into the camera, the viewers saw a close-up of Walstib's eyeball, and then the screen went blank.

CHAPTER 2

Glenn, named after John Glenn, the first American
astronaut to circle the Earth, and his twin sister Sally,
named after Sally Ride, the first female American in space,
were two friendly kids who lived in the small town of
Shepardville, in the middle of the United States.

Their parents were shopping together at the local grocery
store, and when they got to the meat case they both gasped.
"Oh, no," said their mom, "the price of ground beef has
gone up since last week."

"Everything's gone up again," said their dad looking at the
other meats, "chicken, pork, and fish. Thankfully the kids
have been catching quite a lot of cricks lately."

Kids across the country had been catching crickets for
years to supplement the protein portion of their meals, ever
since the price of food had started to skyrocket up. Crickets
have 13 grams of protein per 100 gram serving compared to
14 grams for beef. Not bad to eat if you were imaginative
with your recipe, and, cricks were free.

"I still can't get used to eating crickets."

"I think it's OK, especially if you just call them cricks. You
know there are now upscale restaurants in New York City
that sell cricks as a delicacy."

"Really?"

"Yeah, they roast them with all sorts of flavors like
lavender and honey."

"Maybe we'll try that, if we have to shift to an all cricket
diet."

While their parents shopped, Glenn and Sally were in their
backyard setting up that evening's cricket traps. They had
mixed a little sugar and some old bread crumbs together.

They sprinkled the mixture on the ground and covered it with a single sheet of newspaper. They repeated this process spreading out eight or nine sheets of newspaper. At night the crickets crawled under the paper, ate the mix, and then camped cozily under the paper. The next morning the sleepy crickets were swept up into a plastic container and stored. On nights when it looked like rain, they used plastic two-liter soda bottles placed inside the garage. They would take off the empty soda bottle cap and cut off the top portion of the bottle. They then inverted the top portion and placed the small opening back into the bottle facing down into the bottle then used duct tape to seal the edges together. Then they would place some of the sugar and bread crumb mixture into the bottle, turn it on its side, and placed it in the garage. At night the crickets would jump into the bottle to eat the mix but then couldn't get out. For Glenn, his sister, and most kids in their neighborhood, this had simply become part of their evening and morning chores.

CHAPTER 3

Eddie, in his personalized tie-dye spacesuit, was outside the Space Zoo 1 testing his new jetpack. He was hovering just outside the main windows, and waited for instructions from Jane who was inside.

"Eddie can you hear me?" asked Jane, who was watching Eddie through the main windows.

"Loud and clear, thanks," responded Eddie.

"I'll read from your checklist, and as always, all of your movements will be recorded on the inside monitors so we can analyze what works and what doesn't later on. Ready for the checklist?"

"Let her rip."

"Never say rip when you're in a spacesuit."

"OK, go ahead."

"Come forward one meter, said Jane."

Eddie moved the joystick forward with his thumb and forefinger gingerly, and the jetpack's rear thrusters moved him forward a little bit. He pulled back on the joystick just a hair and the forward thruster came on for a small burst, just enough to stop him.

"Excellent," beamed Jane. "Now back two meters, slowly."

Eddie moved the joystick accordingly.

"Good. Now up three meters, slowly"

Eddie pulled up on the joystick, and he moved up three meters.

"OK, now try turning around in a full circle, slowly."

Task complete.

All the Space Zoo Patrol members on the bridge were watching. The test was going well.

"Very good. Now come forward about ten meters quickly."

Eddie moved the joystick forward all the way and went forward very quickly but when he tried to pull back, the joystick stuck and he crashed into the Space Zoo 1 main windows. His eyes went cross-eyed and his tongue splatted on the inside of the visor on his helmet.

Two junior officers who had been watching on their computer monitors started giggling as they pushed some buttons on their computer.

Jane looked at them and said sternly, "Don't."

One of the junior officers turned his head slightly and said, "Too late."

"You guys," sighed Jane.

"What was that?" asked Eddie.

"Nothing," responded Jane quickly.

As Eddie un-jammed the joystick and hovered back away from the windows, he could see inside. And, to his dismay, he saw on some of the computer screens a close up of his cross-eyed face with his tongue hanging out.

"I'm a screen saver already?" he asked quietly.

"I'm afraid so," Jane said in as friendly a tone as she could manage without laughing.

"Not again," Eddie sighed.

CHAPTER 4

Meanwhile, in Arizona, a bright yellow jet plane raced
down the runway and took off. Not just an ordinary jet, but
a scramjet. NASA had developed the latest in jet engines
and it was fourteen times faster than a regular jet. They
were long and sleek for low air resistance while they were
flying in the atmosphere, but in addition to the scramjet,
they had a laser propulsion system for maneuvering in
space. The Space Zoo Patrol pilots called their jets
Zoomerangs because they went back and forth between the
Earth and their destination, the space station Space Zoo 1.

There were several spaceports in the United States but most
Zoomerang shuttle pilots liked the Arizona site since the
weather was always dry and sunny, making takeoffs and
landings easier. The northern spaceports were snowed in
during winter and the southeast coast spaceports were
closed during hurricane season. Scientists were always
looking for a way to stop hurricanes.
The pilots received hundreds of hours of practice in the
simulator before they actually got an opportunity to launch,
fly, and dock the Zoomerangs. Any wrong maneuver could
be disastrous. So the pilots were very serious about their
work even though it was really fun flying in space.

Commander Prati, an orangutan from Borneo, was named
after Pratiwi Sudarmono, a female NASA space shuttle
payload specialist who was head of the microbiology
department at the University of Indonesia. Commander
Prati guided the Zoomerang 4 toward the Space Zoo 1. She
was always calm and steady, which made her one of the

best pilots in the fleet. Her passengers today were the latest group of Space Zoo Patrol interns.

After they took off, Prati heard the familiar 'urping' noises from first-time passengers. The speed of takeoff combined with the sudden weightlessness made for a sense of motion sickness that few avoided. Prati looked back and asked kindly, "Anyone feel queasy?"

All the passengers were holding their hands to their mouths and their eyes looked a little glazed over. One passenger managed a weak, "We're fine."

"That's what they always say." Prati said under her breath. "There's motion sickness bags in the slots under your seats. Just in case."

"No, no. We're OK," said another passenger.

CHAPTER 5

Eddie and Jane sat in their command seats on the bridge. Jane gazed out at the spinning Earth below and said, "I can't wait for the new interns to show up. I always find it exciting to see the new prospects, hear all about their lives, and how they got interested in science."

Eddie nodded in agreement, "I agree. This is an exciting time for us and an exciting time in their lives, too."

They continued to stare out the main windows in anticipation of the shuttle that would carry the new interns to the orbiting space station.

The phone rang on the command desk, jolting them back to attention. Eddie pushed the speakerphone button so all on the bridge could hear, "Hello, this is Space Zoo 1."

"Hello Captain Eddie, this is Commander Prati of Zoomerang 4. We have you on visual and will be arriving shortly."

"Good to hear from you, Commander," said Eddie. We look forward to your arrival and will meet you at the airlock." Eddie pushed the speakerphone button again to hang up and then pushed the arrival button. The arrival button started a blue blinking warning light. Usually arrivals went smoothly, however, when two ships dock in space there is always room for error and the warning light served to keep everyone alert. In addition, a soft computer voice started announcing the arrival distance: "*4000 meters.*"

Everyone watched intently. The clock on the bridge made a slight clicking sound indicating that a minute had gone by.

"*3950 meters.*"

Another minute clicked by.

"*3900 meters.*"

Eddie fidgeted, "This will take forever."

"It is Commander 'slow and steady' Prati. She's the best, she's never had a docking accident," noted Jane.

"I know," sighed Eddie.

Another click of the clock. "*3850 meters.*"

Eddie stood up, turned to Jane, and said, "We have plenty of time to get a soda at the cafeteria on the way to the docking bay."

Jane stood up and said, "Good idea."

Eddie signaled to Chris and Berty, both Canadian geese and junior officers, "You have the bridge. Please let us know when they get to 500 meters."

The two officers nodded, "Yes, Sir."

Eddie and Jane left the bridge and started walking down the corridor to the cafeteria.

"You know, I never found out what sparked your interest in science," said Jane as she looked over at Eddie.

"Hmm. I guess we've been too busy for much personal discussion since the day we both arrived."

"I'm just curious."

"OK. A long time ago my family had a wonderful dinner that ended with a delicious dessert. You know I like dessert?"

"Yes, I know. Go on."

"My older brother had been excited about making a cake from a new recipe he had seen on a cooking show. My mom asked him if he had written down the recipe. He bragged that he had a great memory and didn't need to write anything down. Later that day, I walked by the kitchen and stopped to watch him start on his cake. He looked very confident as he measured, poured, and whisked all the ingredients. He poured the batter into a cake pan

and put it in the oven. Later, when the timer rang, we both ran back to the kitchen and he pulled out what was supposed to be a super fluffy, kilometer-high cake."
"But?"
"But it was more like a centimeter-high cake. He had forgotten the ingredient that makes the batter rise. He cleaned up and I did a little research. I found that adding baking powder creates bubbles, which make the batter rise. We started over and made the cake together. The new cake ended up making a delicious dessert." Eddie stopped and smiled as if he could still taste the cake. "And I became hooked on researching stuff and figuring out how to make things."
They continued walking, and Jane said, "And that's why you're a great engineer."
"And a baker."
They got to the cafeteria and each took a glass of that day's special - ginger limeade.
As they walked toward the landing dock, Eddie asked, "So how about you?"
"One day in school, also a long time ago, we were playing kickball and it was my turn to be up. I kicked the ball, it went up in the air, and the other team caught it and I was out. The inning was over and I left a runner stranded on second base. I felt bad. The next time I was up we had a runner on third base and only one out." Jane stopped, and with a serious look said, "I figured all I had to do was keep the ball on the ground so the runner could advance to home plate. I just had to change the angle of my foot on the ball, and the ball would stay on the ground. So I kicked the ball soccer style instead of football style. The ball stayed on the ground, the runner made it to home plate, scored a run and we won the game. I ended up really enjoying working with

angles and other mathematical concepts and so became a mathematician."

"And one of the best navigators AND one of the best players on the company kickball team," added Eddie. "Thank you."

Just then Eddie's cell phone announced: "Zoomerang 4 is 500 meters out from Docking Bay E."

"On our way," said Eddie into his cell phone.

CHAPTER 6

Mr. Portlay, the owner of Mega Global Food Corporation, was one of the richest men in the world. He became rich by buying up virtually every grocery store in the world. He had started small by buying old mom and pop corner markets, he organized pickets to drive away their business and then would offer them less than the store was worth as they became desperate to sell. He did the same with small food stores, then local chains, then regional chains, and eventually large national chains. Once he had control over the retail stores he put the squeeze on the farmers to lower their prices. He made a fortune.

Now, Portlay sat at his large desk reviewing paperwork and occasionally looked at the ten TV screens and computer monitors on the wall by his desk. Because he was in the food business, he watched the various news channels, the business channels, agricultural reports, and the weather channels. He loved the food business.

Mr. Portlay also loved food and also watched all the cooking channels. He was, according to all the news reports and celebrity gossip reports, the largest man in the world. Mr. Portlay weighed 680 kilograms. The old record was Jon Minnoch, from the Unites States, who weighed 635 kilograms before he died. Sixteen of the top twenty heaviest men in the world were from the United States.

Across the large room was his financial assistant, Jim Slennar, who sat at another large desk with ten computer monitors. He was tall and slender and, all his friends would agree, had a very pleasant personality. He needed a good personality to put up with Portlay. The last fifteen of his assistants had each quit after working there for less than a month. Slennar was coming up on a full year.

"Slennar," screamed Portlay.

'I'm less than ten meters away,' Slennar said under his breath. "Yes, Sir," he said in cheery voice.

"Anything yet?" asked Portlay.

"Still searching…wait a minute…I think I have it." Slennar spun his chair around. "Your business connections in England were right. A new small grocery store just opened up outside of London."

"Send in a team to negotiate with the owner, buy them out, and then shut it down."

CHAPTER 7

The Zoomerang 4 docked at the Space Zoo 1 without a hitch, as usual.

The outer airlock door opened, which allowed everyone on the Zoomerang to depart and enter the airlock. The outer airlock door closed and the inner airlock door opened and everyone walked forward into the space station. Eddie and Jane stood waiting.

"Permission to come aboard?" asked Commander Prati.

"Of course," responded Eddie cheerfully.

The Commander shook Eddie's paw and Jane's wing. She turned back to her passengers, who were standing in line. The interns were all wearing their new space suits, standard issue white, with each suit hand tailored to fit their individual body types. "Interns, this is Captain Eddie, a beaver from the United States, named after Edwin Aldrin, the U.S. astronaut who was the second man on the moon." Eddie nodded his head. "And this is Navigator Jane, a barn owl from England, named after the famous British animal expert Dr. Jane Goodall."

Jane bowed slightly, and said, "It looks like the launch center did a good job of tailoring your space suits."

The interns stared at Eddie's tie-dye space suit.

"Whaaat?" scoffed Eddie.

"Eddie designs and builds most of the new equipment up here," said Jane. "We gave him a little leeway when he made his own new space suit."

"Let me introduce your new interns," said the Commander. She opened her log book, which detailed everyone who traveled on the Zoomerang.

"These names are in no particular order, I am just reading them off as they were logged in. First up, John."

John stepped forward and lightly waved. "John, a penguin from Antarctica, was named after John Davis, Captain of a sailing vessel and who was the first person to set foot on Antarctica."

Eddie and Jane nodded.

"Marcos."

Marcos stepped forward and smiled. "Marcos, a monkey from Brazil, was named after Marcos Pontes, Brazil's first astronaut."

Eddie and Jane nodded.

"Lu, a panda, was named after Dr. Lu Zhi, the head panda conservationist at Beijing University's Giant Panda Conservation Center."

Lu Lu stepped forward and gave a big grin. "Call me Lu Lu," she said.

Jane said, "Hello Lu Lu."

"Andy."

Andy stepped forward, his tail gave a happy thump. "Andy, a grey kangaroo, was named after Dr. Andy Thomas, one of the Australian astronauts."

Eddie and Jane nodded.

"Liz."

Liz stepped forward and gave a happy smile. "Liz, a koala, was named after Elizabeth Blackburn, a Nobel Prize winner from Australia."

Eddie and Jane nodded.

"Thebe."

Thebe stepped forward and waved. "Thebe, a pygmy hippo, was named after Thebe Medupe, founding Director of Astronomy Africa."

Eddie and Jane nodded.

"Dave and Paul."

Two Golden Retrievers stepped forward, their tails were really wagging. "Sorry, don't have any background listed. Dr. Walstib just asked me to bring them along. I don't know if he meant for me to bring them back or let them stay here."

Eddie and Jane waved and looked surprised. Eddie said, "We'll take care of them up here."

"Then that's it," said the Commander. "As usual, if you could please sign my log book indicating you have received the interns."

Eddie signed the book.

Jane looked at the group, "Commander, why don't you go relax in the Captain's Lounge before your trip back? We've got some home-brewed ginger limeade."

"That sounds good. Thank you." Commander Prati knew her way and headed off.

Jane continued, "Interns, follow us to the conference room."

As they left the docking bay area, all the interns, one by one, dropped their very full motion sickness bags into a large trash can with a sign above it that read, 'Please Deposit All Motion Sickness Bags Here.'

CHAPTER 8

After a quick walk down the hall from the Zoomerang airlock, Jane led the group of interns into a small meeting room. It had a large screen in front and twelve chairs around an oval table in the middle. The interns hurried to find seats. Eddie followed them in and closed the door. Eddie stood in front of the newly arrived group and said, "Welcome to the Space Zoo Patrol Intern Program." Everyone smiled.

"Here, we will expand on your existing scholastic work with two main areas of instruction. The first is Space Habitat Preparedness. These classes will prepare you for the rigors of living and working in space, and will include classes such as, how to sleep, eat, spacewalk, and yes, how to go to the bathroom."

Everyone looked bright-eyed at the idea of a spacewalk and there were a couple of snickers at that last comment.

Jane added, "We also have a gym, which you will use every day. In space, without gravity, you lose muscle and bone density, even after only three to four weeks. So, you will need to exercise to keep up your strength."

Eddie continued, "The second area is to extend your existing knowledge of the main fields of science as they apply to space. These areas, as you know, are math, biology, chemistry, physics, astronomy, and geology. You will learn in the classroom, in the laboratory, and with practical paws-on assignments. A typical day might include class in the morning, lunch, lab experiments in the afternoon, dinner, then free time. Some days we will learn as a group, and some days you will have independent study. This program will be tough, some interns don't actually complete the Program, but it will be loads of fun."

"A few comments about your spacesuits,' said Jane. "You will wear these at all times up here. When you take a spacewalk all you need do is attach your helmet. Also, after these suits were tailored, they were scanned and several additional suits are now being made and will be delivered later."

"The bulk of today will be a tour of the space station," said Eddie. "Space Zoo 1 has two main sections. The central tube where we are now, we call the Core. The Core houses the bridge, the labs, and the control functions of the station. Attached to the Core are the solar panels which provide the electrical energy for the entire station. There is no gravity on the Core, which is why your space suit boots have micro-magnets attached on the soles. The ring that spins around the Core, we call the Wheel, because it looks like a Ferris wheel. It houses the cafeteria, the sleeping quarters, the gym, and the entertainment center. It does provide a sense of gravity."

"Any questions?" asked Jane.

"Yes," said Lu Lu, in a soft voice. "Why is the space station yellow? Most of the other items in space are silver or white."

"That's a good question," responded Jane. "We designed it so that it would be more easily seen from Earth. Studies show that yellow is the easiest color to see from a distance, especially in contrast to the blackness of space."

"Why would you care about the looks of something you are building?" asked John.

"A lot of engineers pay attention to the design elements of a product. It may make it easier to use, or more pleasing to use. Ferdinand Porsche was one of the first auto manufacturers to make his cars sleek and beautiful. Steve Jobs designed his computers and phones to be almost works of art. Plus," she paused, "Walstib thinks it looks cool and he always wants to be able to keep an eye on us." Jane looked around at the interns, "And by the way, we should never be timid about asking questions. It's good to ask questions. What's bad is knowing you don't know something, and not bothering to try to find the answer." Eddie finished up, "Welcome, again. I have to go to the bridge. Jane will escort you to your bunk room where you can drop your gear and old civilian clothes. I'll see you on the bridge where you'll start your tour."

"One more thing," Jane said, as she pushed a button on the remote, "we have the best view of any Internship Program in the world." The large screen at the front of the room clicked on and revealed a live feed of the beautiful spinning Earth below.

Everyone applauded and hooted.

CHAPTER 9

The bunkroom was small, but everyone had a bed next to a window and a closet. After they stowed their gear, Jane led the interns to the bridge.

Jane started the tour, "The bridge is a room where the Space Zoo Patrol members control everything that goes on in the Space Zoo 1. We control the navigation, all the mechanical aspects of the spaceship such as electrical, plumbing, computers, and air conditioning, as well as keeping an eye on all the members when they are in the labs or taking spacewalks to make sure they are safe. The term bridge was originally used for the control area on ships that sailed in the oceans, and continues to be used on spaceships. The computers around the room connect to all the workings of the ship. The two command seats in front of you are for Captain Eddie and me."

Eddie was in one of the seats working at his computer monitor. He waved.

"In front of Eddie are the highest ranking junior officers, both Canadian Geese. Chris, named after Chris Hadfield, a Canadian astronaut, and Berty, named after Roberta Bondar, the first female Canadian astronaut. They help steer the station and keep it in the appropriate orbit. Mostly Low Earth-Orbit, which makes Zoomerang trips easier. But we can move to a higher geosynchronous orbit. It all depends on our needs. They steer the station using our electrically powered laser propulsion system. If we aren't available, they can help." Chris and Berty waved.

Jane continued, "In the front of the room are windows that overlook the Earth below which is always spinning and always beautiful. You may come by anytime you feel homesick, need to feel inspired, or just need to remember why we're here. To the left, on the wall, are 32 computer monitors or TV screens, eight across by four up and down. Each individually shows various scenes such as the labs, the engine compartment, the cafeteria, the hydroponic gardens, and many other areas. Or they can be combined to form one large screen. On the right wall are several small doors that lead to passageways containing electrical wires, air conditioning ducts, and water pipes. And at the back of the room, are regular doors that lead to other parts of the space station."

"Tell them about the shell," said Eddie without looking up. The interns looked intrigued.

"The hull or shell of the station is made of graphene, which is two hundred times stronger than steel, yet lighter and thinner than paper."

The interns' eyes grew wide.

"I know, cool, huh?" said Jane. "It's more expensive than the usual material, but it's so light that we save on the fuel launching it up here."

The interns looked fascinated, but Jane could also hear their stomachs rumbling.

"Next stop is the cafeteria. After which we'll see some of the labs and research rooms, which include the rainforest room, the desert room, and the 3D printer room."

The interns happily followed Jane to the cafeteria.

CHAPTER 10

The next day, in Shepardville, all the neighborhood kids were on their way to school. Some kids took electric buses, some were on motorized skateboards, some on hoverboards, and some walked. Glenn, Sally and their two best friends all arrived at their high school by bicycle. Glenn, Sally and their friends had grown up together, were all on the same science team, and were all on the same swim team. All the students filed into class, the bell rang, and first period started.

Miss Christa, one of the ninth grade government teachers said, "Good morning class," and several hands flew up. Normally, in first period, the students were still wiping the sleepers out of their eyes and it took a while for the students to become engaged. Normally, it took some coaxing to get one hand to raise up.

Slightly shocked, she pointed to one student and said, "Yes, Sally."

"Coming to school this morning, we saw people marching in front of the grocery store with signs. What were they doing?"

"That's called 'picketing.' People picket when they think something is wrong and want the owners of the business or store to change what they are doing. Usually people go talk with the owners first and sometimes the owners change what they are doing. Maybe they just weren't aware of the problem. But sometimes the owners refuse to change. If people are mad enough about an issue, they organize a group of people, make signs that say what they want, and walk back and forth in a line in front of the store. All lined up, holding the signs on top of wooden stakes they look like a picket fence. They hope other people will see the commotion, either in person or on the news, and join them in their cause. Maybe people will call local officials or stop going to the store."

"This is the first time I've ever seen a picket line. Do they happen often?" asked Scott.

"Quite a bit in the past. For example, when people wanted better working conditions, better pay, equal rights, or the right to vote."

"Does it work?" asked Wally.

"In each of the examples I just gave, it worked. And we are all better off for it."

Gordon shot his hand up.

Miss Christa pointed at him.

"One sign said 'Think globally - Act locally.' What does that mean?"

"Maybe the problem is widespread and people realize that the solution has to start somewhere, it might as well start locally. Then maybe others will follow."

The teacher pointed her remote control at the large screen in front of the class and turned on the screen, she clicked a few more times to bring up video examples of picket lines.

"So, as you see, in a democracy, ordinary people can bring about important changes. That is why it is important to keep up with current events, to see if the world is moving forward in a way that is right for everyone. I think I may have reminded you a few times to read the newspaper, read the news on the Internet, or watch the news on TV."

"Maybe a hundred times," someone said from the back of the room. Everyone laughed, including the teacher.

Glenn asked, "One of the signs said, 'Buy Local.' What does that mean?"

"A lot of the buy local debate deals with keeping jobs in the local community. Some countries have lower pay rates than other countries and so their products are cheaper. If we buy those foreign products, we the consumer may save money but the local workers may lose their jobs. In a grocery store a lot of food comes from far away, maybe another state or even from another country. Sometimes the stores have to buy from someplace else just due to nature. For example, if you live in Alaska, you can't grow bananas, so you have to import them from a warmer climate, say Brazil.

Sometimes, for the store, it's cheaper to buy from a big farm that has lower costs, even though that farm may be far away."

Another student raised her hand, "But keeping our food costs low sounds good."

"Many people complain about the quality or taste of food that is shipped from maybe a thousand miles away. If it is a vegetable or fruit it may have been picked too early in order to keep it firm so it doesn't get smushed in shipment. You've all seen tomatoes that may look red on the outside but are never juicy or flavorful on the inside."

Everyone nodded.

"Any more questions about that?"

Everyone shook their heads.

"All right, let's continue with our discussion about the origins of democracy."

CHAPTER 11

At Glenn and Sally's house, it was hot outside, so they were inside in the air conditioning watching TV.

Their mom looked over from the kitchen and said, "Please do your homework."

Glenn and Sally, without looking away from the TV, both said, "We just did."

Trying to feel like she was in charge, their mom said, "Then it's OK to watch some TV."

Without looking away from the TV they both said, "Thank you."

They were tired of watching whatever they were watching and punched the remote to change channels.

"That concludes our in-depth series," said the announcer, "on the seventy-seven things you can do with used tooth picks."

"Not that channel," said mom.

"But it's the happy news," protested Sally.

"I know, but it's all useless stuff, it's just a waste of time."

The announcer continued, "And good news from Hollywood, the long awaited Pinocchio undercover secret agent movie will start filming in a few months. The gag is that he has to tell white lies to keep up his cover, but every time he lies, his nose grows longer. It will be hilarious."

"Change it," said mom. "Try the local news to see what the weather will be tomorrow."

They changed the channel.

"So the coaches and players are ready for a win this weekend. And the fans are too."

"And that was sports. Thanks Michael," said the local news anchor. "Now, let's go live to Janet, our reporter in the field. Janet, what's all the fuss about?"

"Jack, I'm here at the Cross Roads Mini-Mart."

"Mom, Mom, come here," yelled Glenn. "This is what we saw this morning on the way to school."

Their mother dried her hands on a dish towel as she walked over to the TV.

"As you can see behind me, a picket line has formed. Let's hear what they have to say." The reporter walked toward one of the picketers and motioned for her to come over. "Hello ma'am. What's your name?"

The picketer, a tall attractive woman, said, "My name is Pam."

"You look like you have quite a gathering here today. What would you like to tell the viewers?"

"We've all been coming here for years. We like the place, and we have always liked the owner. However, he just sold his store to a new owner. The new owner has replaced all the locally grown vegetables with vegetables from another country. They're hardly ever ripe and the prices have gone up as well."

"That sounds awful. What does the new owner say?"

"They won't talk with us."

"That sounds bad, too. But we thank you for talking with us here at Local News One. It seems we're at a stalemate here. We'll keep covering the story. Back to you in the studio."

"That does sound bad. I'm afraid that's happened all too often lately. But for now, turn off the TV and please go get some cricks for dinner," said Mom.

"What happens to the local farmers if they can't sell their vegetables?" asked Sally.

"I don't know."

"What don't you know? I thought you knew everything," said Glenn and Sally's dad who just came home from work. Mom and Dad kissed.

"We just saw on the news that the local Cross Roads Mini Mart is being picketed for dropping their local farmers," said Mom.

"What happens to the local farmers if they can't sell their vegetables?" asked Sally again.

"They might go out of business," responded Dad.

"How many local farmers are there?" asked Sally, sounding concerned.

"I don't know," said Dad.

"I'll ask my teacher tomorrow," said Glenn.

"She'll probably know," said Mom. "Now Glenn, please go get some cricks to add to dinner. And Sally can you please set the table?"

Sally started to set the table and Glenn went out to the backyard.

Outside in the backyard was what they called the 'crick pantry.' It was formally the garden tool shed and was large enough to hold several thousand crickets in plastic containers. Glenn's parents liked to keep the pantry well stocked in case there were times when they couldn't collect any crickets.

Glenn opened the pantry door and found that it was totally empty. He shouted, "Mom! Dad! Come quick!"

In a few moments both parents came running. "What?" they both asked.

Glenn held open the doors and said, "Look, it's empty."

"Oh no," said Mom. "This took a lot of work to collect. I'm so sorry, honey."

"Who would steal cricks?" asked Dad, sounding mystified. He pulled out his cell phone and called the police.

"Hello, Metro Police," said the desk sergeant. "How can I help you?"

"Our crick pantry has been broken into. Everything's gone."

"Anything else missing?" inquired the sergeant.

"No, just the cricks. This will cost us a small fortune if we have to buy this much meat at the store."

"We'll send an officer over to fill out a report. This is very strange. This is the fifth reported crick theft this week in your neighborhood." Glenn's dad turned off his phone.

Glenn looked at his parents, "What's going on?"

His mom said, "I don't know. That's a good question."

"Dad?"

"This is new to me too. Ask at school tomorrow."

CHAPTER 12

The next morning Glenn was even more eager to get to school than usual. As soon as the bell sounded and everyone was seated, Glenn threw his hand up. Their teacher said, "Yes, Glenn."

"Miss Christa, our cricks were stolen yesterday. Why would someone steal cricks? Why is the cost of food going up? Why is there less food these days? Has it always been this way?" asked Glenn.

Several of the other students mentioned that they had their cricks stolen as well.

"The short answer is that there used to be more farmland," replied Miss Christa.

The students leaned forward a bit, there was obvious interest in this subject.

"I take it that you would like a little more than the short answer."

The students nodded.

"Good, if there is one thing that I'd like you to learn this year, it is to never be satisfied with the short answer. The teacher pointed her remote at the large screen again.

"Hundreds of thousands of years ago early people were nomadic hunters." The remote clicked, and an illustration of cave men hunting woolly mammoths appeared on the screen. "Then about 10,000 years ago, humans grew their first crop, which was wheat." She clicked and an illustration of Egyptians farming wheat appeared on the screen. "Hundreds of years ago, most people were involved in farming." Click, and an illustration of a farmer plowing a field in Virginia appeared on the screen. "Some people made pottery or were blacksmiths, but most grew at least some of their own crops. However, with the invention of farm machinery, such as the first gas powered tractor in 1892 in Iowa, farmers realized they could farm very large farms quickly instead of using slow animals to plow the fields." Click, and a picture of an old tractor tilling the ground appeared. "So some people bought out other people's small farms to create larger farms, and people who didn't want to be farmers could sell their farms."

"Why would somebody sell their farm?" asked Scott.

"Farming is a tough life. You get up early and stay up late. Small family farms didn't make all that much money. So when it was time for the original farmers to retire, many of their children sold their farms. This allowed them to go into areas that they preferred, such as manufacturing, or writing, or medicine."

Miss Christa looked at her students. Their eyes weren't glazing over yet, so she continued, "Machinery and large farms opened up a whole new era of economical farming. By 1970, in the United States, eighty percent of our food came from the largest farms. Farming became a business instead of a family tradition. And like most businesses, some failed, some grew, and some companies bought up other companies. In the United States, there have been over 1,000 car companies over the years, now there are only about ten. In the past, there were about two million family farms. Now, ninety nine percent of all food comes from one company, the Mega Global Food Corporation."

"What happened to all the small farms? I don't see any around here," said Kathryn.

"Some farms were too small to be economical. The farmers would have to haul their tractors from one small lot to the next, so it would end up being unproductive. When the small farmers sold out, some farms were merged to form bigger farms, but many farms simply became building sites. As populations grew, and more people moved to the cities, the cities expanded into suburbs, and builders built more houses, malls, offices, and factories. All of it covers old family farms, including where we all live now. New Jersey was the first state to be more than half covered by manmade material. Many other states have also gone in the same direction."

"Should we let people sell their land to someone who's going to do whatever they want with it?" asked Wally.

"Do any of you want to bulldoze your house and turn it back into a small farm?

Everyone shook their heads no.

"The solutions are not as simple as we'd like them to be."

"But if bigger is more economical to run, why have the food prices gone up so much?" asked Judy.

"It's called greed. And when you are a monopoly, you control everything. And that's bad. More companies meant more competition and new ideas and new products sprang up. But the food company owner convinced the elected officials that there is nothing new in growing crops and competition just means added expense in advertising and extra people to run different companies. The food company owner told them not to interfere when he wanted to buy up a small farm. And they didn't."

"What convinced them?" asked Gus.

"We'll discuss bribery during our ethics class," said the Miss Christa. Click, and an old picture popped up of a large businessman pushing a pile of money across the desk to an elected official.

"But if we run out of farm land, where will we get our food?" asked Glenn.

"Well that's the question. Isn't it? No one seems to be thinking about this."

After class, Glenn gathered his friends and said, "I've been thinking about this. We've got to help."

Sally said, "I agree."

Mario, named after Mario Molina, a chemist from Mexico who was a Nobel Prize winner said, "Me too."

Kali, named after Kalpana Chawla, the first woman from India in space, said. "But how?"

"Let's get together this weekend. Bring your bikes and your helmet-cams to my house. I have an idea."

CHAPTER 13

The Mega Global Food Corporation headquarters was a big building set in the middle of a field of corn. On the outside it was designed to look like a paper shopping bag. The owner of the company, Mr. Portlay, thought it would be clever. The architect did not. However, what Mr. Portlay wanted, Mr. Portlay got. The outside was covered in exotic blonde woods to match the color of a paper bag. The trouble with using rare exotic wood is that usually exotic means almost extinct. Mr. Portlay didn't care, he had the wood smuggled into the country in his food container ships from sites around the world.

The reporter from the Global Agricultural Journal just shook her head every time she looked at the building when she came to interview Mr. Portlay. She went up the elevator to the top floor and knocked on Portlay's office door, which was twice the size of a regular door. Slennar let her in. "Hey Jim. How are you?" asked the reporter.

"I'm fine, thanks Rachel. Right this way," he said as he escorted the reporter over to Portlay's desk. Rachel was named after Rachel Carson, the author of the influential agricultural book *Silent Spring*.

Portlay was watching his computer screens with his back to the room. He was eating at his desk, as usual, this time it was two large lobsters. He turned around to see the reporter, or rather his desk chair turned for him. It was more like half a sofa and was made of very sturdy steel to accommodate his size. He controlled it with a control knob on one of the chair arms. "Hello, Rachel. What pressing questions do you have for me today?"

"The editors want to know how your sales and profits will do this quarter. As you know, the industry financial quarterly reports are all due next week and we hoped to get a jump on the other news outlets."

Portlay waved his fork, "Join me in some lobster dipped in melted butter with a touch of sea salt and honey while we talk shop?"

"Oh, no thanks, I already had lunch."

"So did I. This is just a snack before dinner."

"It looks delicious, but still, no thanks Mr. Portley."

Portlay looked furious. He put down his fork. "It's Port-lay not Port-ley. Portlay is of French origin, my grandparents came to New Orleans decades ago. Portley means fat. I am not fat, I am just big boned. The kids at school teased me and called me Portley. I couldn't do anything about it then, but I won't put up with it now. Get out of my office."

"I'm sorry, Sir. It was an honest mistake."

"Get out."

Slennar escorted her back to the door, and as he let her out, he whispered, "Not to worry. It happens all the time. He'll get over it and you can come back tomorrow."

"Thanks, Jim."

They could both hear Portlay as he screamed, "Slennar, get me another lobster."

CHAPTER 14

Eddie stood at the front of Lab 2 as the new interns filed in. Labs 1, 3, and 4 were already in use that day.

"Before we start our work in the laboratory, it is important to know how new knowledge is discovered. Understanding this will help guide us in our experiments. In science, we use the scientific method to get knowledge. Within the scientific method, there are two approaches, basic research and applied research. Basic research is when you just want to poke around and see what you see, like when you say 'Hey, what's that?' You should always explore and observe those things that interest you, whether you are in or out of the classroom. These investigations should be fun and exciting."

"What's the second?" asked Liz.

"The second approach," continued Eddie, "is applied research. It is a more detailed approach to follow when you want to find something out that is more specific. For example, 'Can we make a car battery that lasts longer?' or 'Can we make a faster jet engine?' There is a process for this method. First you make a best guess, or a temporary explanation, called a hypothesis. Then you ask questions, or conduct research in the library or in the field, or conduct a test or trial run, or conduct an experiment, which we will do here in the laboratory. Then you write down all the answers you get. This is your information or what we call data. Then you compare the data to the hypothesis to see if you have answered the original question or solved the problem."

"Does the experiment always work?" asked Lu Lu.

"Sometimes you find the answer right away and sometimes you have to keep trying new experiments, which may take another day or several years. You've used WD40, the popular lubricant spray?"

Everyone nodded.

"At first, the company tried many different formulas for the spray. The first 39 tries failed. The 40th attempt finally worked, hence the name."

Jane stepped forward, "OK, let's take a tour of the lab."

Jane and Eddie spent the next several hours showing the interns all the lab equipment.

Afterwards, they all went to the cafeteria together and discussed ideas for the first set of lab experiments that the interns would start on the next day.

"No, no, no," sighed Lu Lu.

"What's wrong?" asked Liz.

"I had an idea and then I just forgot it."

"I know, I hate that. It happens to me sometimes, too," said Andy.

"Ideas are like dreams, one minute they are there and the next second they are gone," said John.

"It happens to scientists, songwriters, book writers, inventors, chefs, just about everybody," added Jane.

"Why does that happen?" asked Marcos.

Jane cocked her head sideways, "We don't know. But I have a good way to keep from forgetting things."

"What's that?" everyone asked.

"I have a notepad in my suit pocket, a notepad by my bed, at my desk, and in the bathroom," responded Jane.

Everyone giggled.

"No really, sometimes my best ideas come when I'm in the bathroom."

Everyone giggled again.

Jane blushed, "I mean, you know, in the shower."

"That's what we all thought," said Eddie.

"Anyway, if you don't write it down, it's lost," said Jane.

"Sometimes I have a dream so real, when I wake up I know I'll never forget it. And yet minutes later it's gone for good," said Thebe.

"I wonder how many incredible inventions were thought of and then forgotten?" asked John. "Maybe thousands. Plus, I wonder how many inventions have been lost because they don't get the proper funding for manufacturing, distribution, and marketing," added Eddie.

"It's a miracle that anything actually ever gets made or sold," said Jane.

"Or, lots and lots and lots of really hard work," said Eddie.

"Yes, that's the trick," concluded Jane.

"Where do most of the ideas for inventions come from?" asked John.

"Hard to say," responded Eddie. "People are thinking all the time. People at universities, corporations, government agencies, people watching TV, or people figuring something out in a basement or a garage. Several famous computer companies were started in a garage. The Wright Brothers figured out the airplane in their bicycle shop."

"Or in the shower," laughed Marcos.

Eddie summed it up, "The key is to keep thinking."

"And as I say, 'Dream it up - Write it down,' " said Jane.

After lunch, the interns went back to the lab to start tinkering on their ideas. Then to the gym, and then to dinner where they discussed which experiment they should work on first.

CHAPTER 15

The next morning Eddie and Jane were already in the lab as the interns came in.

"Are you ready to get to your first experiment?" asked Jane.

Andy said, "Yes."

Marcos said, "Sure am."

Everyone else nodded.

Eddie put his paw up to his ear, and shouted like a sports coach, "I can't hear you!"

All the interns screamed "Yeah!"

"That's better," said Eddie. He thumped his tail, "Let's solve some problems."

Eddie and Jane left the lab and the interns got started. Knowing of the water shortage on Earth, they had decided to try to create a sweater made of sustainable material that would not have to be washed. They went to the rainforest room and gathered some materials. When they came back they first tried sewing together some large leaves, however, the thread ripped through the soft leafy material. Then they tried weaving together a cloth made from vines. It was way too stiff. Next they made a poncho by cutting a large hole in the center of a large piece of moss. They stitched the sides together using a thin strips of the vines, thin enough to be flexible, yet thick enough to not pull through the moss.

Andy pulled off the top of his spacesuit and tried it on, "It fits OK. It's a little scratchy."

"But it looks nice. You look good in green." said Liz.

They hadn't realized how many hours had slipped by until Eddie and Jane walked in. The interns snapped to attention.

"Hello everyone," said Jane.

Everyone said hello.

Jane said, "Who took the lead on your experiment?"

Andy and Liz stepped forward.

Eddie said, "Show us what you've completed so far."

Andy looked a little nervous, going first, so he looked at the other interns. They all nodded encouragement. He looked back at Eddie and Jane, then said, "We've developed a sweater made from live moss. Moss absorbs the body's dead skin cells and perspiration. Thus, you won't need to shower as often, and you won't waste water."

Liz added, "Plus, during cold weather it naturally tightens and holds in heat. And, during hot weather it naturally loosens and lets out heat."

Andy proudly held up the sweater, "Try it on."

Jane tried on the sweater, "It's a little scratchy, and, it looks a little pale. Healthy moss should be dark green." She took it off and handed it back to Andy.

Liz said, "Oh. It was darker when we got it from the rainforest room."

Eddie asked, "Do you know why that is?"

Andy responded, "No."

"What's your next step?" asked Jane.

"More research," said Andy quietly.

"That's always a good next step," said Eddie.

Liz said. "We'll discuss it over lunch."

Jane and Eddie headed out.

The interns were about to leave when Andy said, "Hey, you guys head to the cafeteria, I have to run an errand, I'll join you in a minute."

Everyone but Andy headed to the cafeteria. Andy went in a different direction.

After a few minutes Andy joined them wearing the sweater and said, "Figured it out."

"It's inside out," Thebe pointed out.

Andy smiled and filled his lab partners in on his new findings while they ate lunch.

After lunch they headed back to the lab.

They saw the sweater was turning a darker green and realized that Andy was on the right track. They realized they didn't have to do any more research and so relaxed and continued their discussion about the movie they had watched the night before.

After a while, the lab intercom crackled and Eddie asked, "Are you all ready for a second evaluation?"

They all shouted "Yes, Sir."

"Excellent. See you shortly."

After a few minutes, Eddie and Jane showed up. They saw the dark green sweater and smiled.

Jane said, "Now I'll try it on." She took off the top half of her spacesuit and tried it on, then gave a little modeling twirl, "Comfy."

"What made the difference?" asked Eddie.

Andy spoke up, "Originally I made the assumption that moss absorbed water through the roots, like other plants. So we made the sweater with the rough side inside so it could absorb the perspiration. Not only did it not absorb water but it was itchy. So I found out that moss absorbs water through its 'leaves' or the outer mossy part. The underneath part is only rough so it can cling onto trees and rocks."

Liz added, "Having the rough part on the outside also makes the sweater more durable."

Jane asked, "How did you get this new information?"

"Hundreds of hours of exhaustive research," smiled Andy.

"Over a one hour lunch?" asked Jane and cocked her head.

"Or maybe I simply walked down to the rainforest room and asked the botanist. It took about five minutes."

"Amazing. Information from a living being," smiled Eddie.

Jane handed the sweater back to Liz. "Congratulations on a wonderful first experiment," she said to the group.
Eddie and Jane headed back to the bridge. The interns headed to the gym for a couple hours of a hard workout and then back to the cafeteria for dinner.

CHAPTER 16

The next day, the interns broke off for individual study or teamed up with a senior or junior officer to learn about the various functions of the space station. Eddie spent most of the day teaching John about the Space Zoo 1's controls. Eddie sat in the Captain's chair and John sat in the Navigator's chair next to Eddie, where Jane normally sat. At the end of the day, Eddie said, "That was a lot of information. Do you think you know all the controls?"
"Yes, Sir, I think I do," said John.
They both relaxed a little and admired the view.
Eddie leaned over a little, "Is it me, or is it cold up here?"
John looked a little baffled, "We're in space. Isn't it always cold up here? I heard your last assignment was in Brazil. Maybe you just got used to being in a hot climate. Personally, I like the cold, it's the wind I can't stand. Did you ever visit the Antarctic?
"No, but I heard it's windy."
"It's really windy."
"As windy as a politician?"
"No, not that windy," John laughed. "Anyway, I like it up here."
"Well I'm getting goosebumps."
Chris and Berty sat in their usual seats, just in front of the two command seats, watching their computer monitors. They had overheard Eddie's comment.
Chris said, "What's wrong with goosebumps?"
Berty said, "I dunno. They're OK with me."
Eddie looked at Chris, "Maybe we could turn up the heat one or two degrees. Please."
Chris turned and said, "You're the boss. I'm not going to get in a 'heated' debate with you."

Berty smiled and said, "It was a civil request. He wasn't being 'hot headed.' "

Eddie looked at John, rolled his eyes and said, "That was a good session. Let's head to dinner."

As they got up to leave, Berty said, "If it gets any hotter, I'll start laying hard boiled eggs."

"Hurry," Eddie said to John.

CHAPTER 17

The next morning after breakfast, the interns again entered Lab 2, where they started working on their second experiment. They spent several hours cutting metal and making boxes. They tried different grinding motors and tubing of various sizes. They tried a few types of compressors and heating units. Thebe and Marcos went to collect buckets of leftover food waste from the cafeteria. They finally got it all put together just as Eddie and Jane entered.

The interns snapped to attention.

"Hello all," said Jane. "Who are the leads for today's experiment?"

John and Lu Lu stepped forward.

Eddie said, "Tell us about your experiment."

Lu Lu said, "We need more soil for our Rain Forest Room up here in Space Zoo 1. It's a whole lot cheaper to make the compost here than shipping it up from Earth."

Eddie and Jane looked at the big silver box.

John proudly stated, "Our quick-composter uses pressure to process left over food like banana peels, apple cores, and egg shells into compost. But instead of waiting weeks or months, this will make compost in seconds. On Earth, cooks use pressure cookers to make meat tender in minutes and the paper industry uses pressure and heat to break down wood fibers to make paper."

Eddie said, "Sounds promising. Show us how it works."

We just finished tinkering," said John. "We don't know if it works."

"This isn't the final exam. Show us what you've done so far."

John passed out safety goggles to everyone, explaining, "As always, when working with items under pressure, you must wear safety goggles."

Everyone put them on.

Lu Lu loaded a bucket of garbage into one end of the machine, and flicked the switch. The machine shook, rattled, and rolled. Compost started coming out the other end.

John happily announced, "It's actually making soil."

Everyone smiled. Then the machine started to grind and make rude burping noises. They all took one step back. The machine started to make louder noises. Everyone took a few more steps back.

Eddie, having seen many an experiment go bad, said, "Maybe someone should turn this off."

Lu Lu took several steps toward the composter, and just as she got close, one of the plastic tubes exploded, hurling garbage all over her. Lu Lu and John looked down at the floor feeling embarrassed.

John said, "We'll discuss it at lunch."

"Right after I take a quick shower," said Lu Lu.

Lu Lu took a shower to wash off all the food debris and changed into her newly arrived extra space suit, then joined the other interns at lunch.

"Did you all figure out anything about how to fix the composter?" Lu Lu asked.

John said, "We haven't come up with anything."

Andy stated, "We think that there was too much pressure in the system. But we also think that we need that much pressure to make the food waste compost quickly."

"So I think we need to add a pressure release valve," said Lu Lu. "As you all probably know, a pressure release valve is made to release just enough pressure, or steam, to keep the container from blowing up but keep most of the pressure in to do the work."

"Exactly," said John. "She's right. A pressure cooker in a kitchen has a pressure release valve. The whistle on a steam train releases a little pressure from the boiler to blow the whistle."

Marcos smiled, "If you held the whistle on for a long enough time, the pressure would all go out and the train would stop." He pretended that he was pulling a train whistle and whistled. "That's why the train conductor doesn't play music on the whistle while he drives from one town to the next."

Everyone stared at Marcos.

"Sorry. I'll focus.

"Lu Lu, when did you think of that?" asked Liz.

"In the shower. Seems Jane was right when she said you could think it up in the bathroom," responded Lu Lu.

"But, I thought she really meant..." said Thebe.

"Nope, apparently she meant shower," said Lu Lu.

They all went back to the lab and rebuilt the quick-composter, adding a pressure release valve this time.

Later that afternoon, Eddie and Jane walked back into Lab 2.

Eddie said solemnly, "Show us."

John again handed out safety goggles to Eddie and Jane. The interns were already wearing theirs. Lu Lu scooped another bucket of food waste into the funnel end of the machine and pushed the button. The machine sputtered. Lu Lu and John still looked a little nervous. A little excess steam puffed out of the pressure release valve on top.

Lu Lu pointed to the pressure release valve and whispered to Eddie and Jane, "PRV."

Eddie and Jane nodded.

A whistle tooted. Marcos smiled, that was his addition.

Then compost came out of the other end.

Eddie said, "Congratulations! That will be a big help up here. See you all at dinner."

Eddie and Jane turned to leave. The interns all high-fived each other.

CHAPTER 18

As Eddie and Jane were about to leave the lab, Jane turned
around in the doorway and said,
"This was a good experiment guys. When at first things go
wrong, you needn't look so sheepish."
Jane then turned into the hallway where Eddie was waiting
and came face to face with two junior officers who were
sheep from New Zealand. Both named after famous New
Zealanders. Betty, was named after Beatrice Tinsley who
had a Ph.D. in cosmology, and Brian, was named after
Brian Mason who had a Ph.D. in geochemistry.
Betty said, incredulously, "Sheepish?"
"Sorry," said Jane. "It's just an expression."
Brian said, "Really?"
Jane, sensing that the sheep were making a mountain out of
a mole hill, said, "Yes, when someone is embarrassed, they
hang their heads and look down. You know, like sheep do
when they spend ninety percent of their day grazing on
grass."
Betty said, "Oh, zing. We carry our weight around here. At
least we don't spend ninety percent of our day turning our
head in circles."
Eddie said, "All right you two. You've each said the same
zingers a hundred times."
Betty said, "See you at dinner, Jane."
Jane said, "All right. See you later."
As they walked in different directions, Jane asked Eddie,
"Do I really turn my head a lot?"
Eddie looked at Jane and turned his head to the left, then to
the right, then to the left, and said, "I don't know," then to
the right, "I'll have to think about it."
"If I look straight ahead at someone, they think I've locked
in on them like they're prey, and I'm about to swoop down

and snatch them up." Jane stared straight at Eddie, her feathers ruffled slightly, and her wings started to spread out.

Eddie gulped and said, "Yeah, turning your head in circles is OK."

CHAPTER 19

After an independent study day, the interns were back at work in Lab 2. For their next experiment, they continued to look for ways that would save water. On their space station tour they had visited the hydroponics garden. 'Hydro' was ancient Greek meaning 'water' and 'ponics' meant 'labor.' So water in tubes carried the nutrients to the plants, attached to the tubes by mini trellises. The water doing the work of carrying nutrients to the plants instead of the soil. In a plastic tube, the water couldn't leach down into the soil, and it couldn't evaporate, thus saving water two ways. In the garden, was a small row of hydroponically grown tomatoes. The tomato plants were a beautiful red and were a healthy size. But the interns had decided that they could grow them bigger. They spent all morning building the tube structure, adding water pumps, attaching already started tomato seedlings from the garden, and adding nutrients to the water.

Eddie and Jane entered and the interns, as usual, snapped to attention.

Jane said cheerfully, "Hello."

They all nodded.

Jane continued, "Who are the leads on this experiment?"

Marcos and Thebe stepped forward.

Eddie said, "Show us what you've completed so far."

Thebe started, "As you know, the water shortage on Earth continues to get worse. However, plants grown hydroponically, meaning without soil, use water very efficiently. The water runs through a plastic trough and the roots hang down into the water where they absorb the fertilizer we add to the water."

Marcos added, "We thought improving on our hydroponic gardens would be helpful up here, and on Earth."

Thebe turned and added more fertilizer to the hydroponic trough, "We've developed a fast acting fertilizer by mixing fertilizer with carbonated water. It adds fertilizer, water, and oxygen at the same time.

Marcos whispered to Thebe, "I already added fertilizer this morning."

Thebe looked at Eddie and Jane. "If some is good then more is better. Right?" he said, sounding hopeful.

Marcos said, "The lack of gravity already allows the vegetables to grow faster than normal. However, we don't know what an extra dose of fertilizer is going to do."

John stated softly, "I added fertilizer this morning when you were gluing the tubes."

Andy, in barely a whisper, said, "I put some in too, when you were adding the pumps."

Eddie and Jane looked at each other and raised their eyebrows.

All of a sudden, the tomatoes started to grow a bit bigger. Then a little larger. Then they were the size of beach balls. Then they made a 'pfffft' sound and split and oozed onto the floor.

Jane looked over at the mess and let out a dejected sigh, "Whoooo."

Eddie, who also stared at the tomato mess and wasn't paying attention to Jane, leaned over to Jane and said, "What?"

Jane said, "Oh, nothing."

"You said something."

"Who?

"You."

"What?"

Eddie said, "That's what I asked. What?"

Jane sounded exasperated, "I don't know. Why are you asking me?"

"What don't you know?"

"If I knew what I didn't know, then I would know what I knew. Is that what you asked?"

Eddie shook his head, "Never mind."

Eddie looked at the interns and said, "We'll let you all figure this out over lunch. See you later this afternoon."

The interns cleaned up the mess quickly, and then headed out. When they arrived at the cafeteria the lunch special sign read, 'Today's Lunch Special - Pasta and All You Can Eat Tomato Sauce.'

They all groaned.

During lunch, the nterns discussed all the possibilities as to what went wrong. After lunch, they hurried back to the lab to start over.

After several hours of work, they finished their second attempt.

Eddie and Jane came in and Marcos and Thebe stood in front of their experiment.

Jane asked, "What went wrong?"

Thebe said, "We didn't know who was feeding the plants and when. So we added a chart to keep track of the feeding schedule."

Marcos added, "Also, our formula for the fertilizer was too strong, so we scaled back the fertilizer a bit."

Eddie said, "Show us."

Marcos and Thebe stepped aside. Eddie and Jane saw a row of tomatoes, ripe, red, and the size of basketballs.

Eddie exclaimed, "Excellent!"

Eddie and Jane started to walk out, and as they got to the door, Andy turned quickly to high five Thebe. Andy's tail hit a tomato and everyone heard a big splat. Marcos and Thebe jumped back in front of the experiment. Jane continued to walk through the door. Eddie stopped at the door for a second but didn't turn around. He smiled and kept walking. When he caught up to Jane, he said, "Should we tell the cafeteria to make pasta and the all-you-can-eat tomato sauce the special again for dinner?"

Jane smiled, "No, but that was funny at lunch."

CHAPTER 20

The next day, the interns were in the conference room for an all-day seminar as they listened to Eddie and Jane describe how to conduct a spacewalk. Spacewalks were an essential task used to make repairs or additions to the outside of the space station.

The following day was an individual training day. All the interns, except John, were in the cafeteria having breakfast. "Marcos, are you nervous about your introductory spacewalk today after lunch?" asked Thebe.
"A little. Why do you ask?" responded Marcos.
"No reason. I would think everyone would be a little nervous before their first one. You just seemed distracted during yesterday's briefing."
"Maybe a little nervous," said Marcos softly.
"You might have missed the part where they said you should have a soda before your walk," said Thebe.
"No. I didn't catch that."
"Here, I'll get you one," smiled Thebe.
Thebe got up, walked over to the soda dispenser, and poured a soda. He came back and handed the soda to Marcos.
"They said the sugar and the caffeine help you stay alert during the walk."
"That makes sense," said Marcos and then downed the soda. "Thanks."
"No trouble at all. Good luck on the walk. We'll be watching."
"Yeah, good luck," said Lu Lu.
"Have fun," added Liz.

Marcos got up, took his tray to the counter, and walked away to the airlocks.

Lu Lu looked at Thebe, "They didn't say that."

"I know," said Thebe. "This will teach him to pay attention."

"Just to be sure for when we go out," said Andy. "They said the opposite."

"That's right. They said don't drink soda. Come on, let's go watch."

They got up, took their trays to the counter, and headed for the bridge.

They got to the bridge just in time to see Eddie leading Marcos out of the station for his first spacewalk. Everyone on the bridge could hear the spacewalk chatter over the intercom.

Eddie and Marcos went through the usual introductory routine, forward, backward, etc. Then everyone heard a little 'toot' coming from Marcos's space suit. Marcos's nose scrunched up. Then a slightly louder 'toot." Marcos pushed the joystick on the jetpack and turned around to see the other interns on the bridge laughing. He turned back to Eddie and said, "I think I missed the part about soda in yesterday's briefing."

"Oh yes," said Eddie. "The part where we said don't drink carbonated beverages before a spacewalk. Because the carbonation inside the body builds up pressure and when you are outside the space station you have a slightly lower pressure inside your space suit. The body's gasses have nowhere to go but out," Eddie said as he tried not to laugh and pretended not to have heard the slight noise in his helmet speakers. "Why do you ask?"

"No reason," said Marcos, as he made a mental note to somehow get even with Thebe.

CHAPTER 21

During the same individual training day, John had been shadowing, or following, Jane to learn more about the daily routines of the space station. It was the end of a long and tiring day. Jane sat in her normal chair, and John got to sit in Eddie's chair, a rare treat.

They were sitting and relaxing in the command chairs when Chris turned to Jane and said, "Hey, isn't it time to make the announcement?"

Jane looked at the clock, "Yes, thanks for reminding me." Jane turned to John and said, "I almost forgot. As you know, Eddie usually makes the 'lights out' announcement every night at 22:00 hours. In the old days that would be 10 PM, but on the space station we adopted the 24-hour clock notation as it is now used in every country."

Jane pulled up the microphone from her chair arm and said, "Attention Space Zoo Patrol. Another great day. It's 22:00 hours, time to turn in. Looking forward to working with you tomorrow. Out."

"I've heard that announcement every night since I've been up here. We all have clocks in our rooms, so why do you make it?"

"Studies have shown that getting a good night's sleep is one of the healthiest and most productive things you can do. This place is filled with smart and hard-working scientists. They'd stay up all night in the labs if we let them. The announcement is just a reminder to not stay up all night."

"Where is Captain Eddie? How come he isn't here to make the announcement?" asked John.

"He's staying up all night in his lab," sighed Jane.

The security drone slowly circled the space station and sent back video images to the big screen on the bridge. Jane and John saw, one by one, the lights go out on Space Zoo 1, all except Lab 51.

CHAPTER 22

The next day, the interns were in Lab 3, as it had airlocks. As usual, Eddie and Jane walked in just before lunch. The interns came to attention.

Jane said, "Good after morning."

Everyone looked at Jane, including Eddie.

"It's my new expression. We have 'good morning' and we have 'good afternoon,' but we don't have any saying for the time between morning and noon. So there it is."

Everyone nodded.

"So, who are the leads today?"

Dave and Paul stepped forward.

Eddie asked, "What's your experiment?"

Dave said, "We are going to prove that gravity is affected by weight. We both agree that it just makes sense that heavier objects would fall faster. And that lighter objects would fall slower. Or, in space, the heavy objects would fall to Earth and the lighter ones would just float."

Paul said, "We call our experiment 'Will It Float?' "

Eddie and Jane looked quizzically at each other, and then at the other interns.

All the other interns in the back either shook their heads, closed their eyes, or put their paws up in disbelief.

Jane said, "OK. Let's see a demo."

As the Retrievers started their experiment, they also started to sing to each other. They sang, "Will it float? Will it float?" to the tune of the 'Will it Float?' skit on the old *Late Night with David Letterman* TV show. "Will it float? Will it float?" they continued.

Dave picked up a wrench from the lab table, put it into the Lab 3 airlock, and pushed the first button. The airlock inner door closed. He pushed the second button, and the outer airlock door opened. Through the lab window they saw the wrench eject into space. He closed the outer door.

Paul said eagerly, "It didn't fall back to Earth. Not heavy enough. Try again."

Dave picked up a sledge hammer, and went through the same airlock procedure.

Through the window they saw the sledge hammer eject into space. "Will it float? Will it float?"

Dave groused, "I thought this one would surely sink. It was pretty heavy."

Eddie said, "Well whaddaya know? It floats."

Dave said excitedly, "Hey, our luck has to change…the first seven items we tested before you got here all floated. Maybe the next one will sink."

Eddie wasn't amused, "Science doesn't rely on luck. Keep trying though. You'll think of something."

As Eddie and Jane left the lab, Eddie turned to Jane and said, "I hope Walstib knows what he's doing."

"I'm sure he has his reasons."

Changing the subject, Eddie said, "How about 'Good before noon'?"

"That just sounds silly."

Dave said, "You all go on to lunch. We'll keep working on this."

Liz tried to sound encouraging, "Are you sure you don't need our help?"

Paul said, "We came up with the idea, we worked on it all morning by ourselves. We want to see this through."

"We'll be in the cafeteria if you need us," said Andy.

The interns went to lunch and tried to figure out how to turn this experiment around. They were stumped. When they returned, half the lab tools were missing. They looked out the window and, sure enough, they were all floating just outside the airlock.

Eddie and Jane walked in just after lunch, apparently not feeling that waiting till later in the day would change the outcome of the experiment. The two Retrievers stood in front of the airlock.

Eddie said, "Show us."

Dave said, "We got the heaviest object we could find." He pushed the button and the outer airlock door opened. A large upright piano drifted out. "Will it float? Will it float?" they sang.

Jane said, "Oh, no."

Paul said, "Oh yes. Certainly this has to fall."

The piano continued to drift and obviously did not fall. The two Retrievers looked at each other in disbelief.

Dave said, "We've failed. Absolutely everything we've sent out hasn't fallen to Earth. No matter how heavy." Silence.

Paul's tail started to wag, "Wait a minute." He turned his back to Eddie and Jane and whispered to Dave. After a minute, Dave nodded. Paul turned to face Eddie and Jane, "We were trying to prove that heavier objects in space would sink, or fall to Earth. However, we feel that we just proved that all objects, no matter how heavy, will float in space, and given the proper distance won't feel the pull of gravity."

Dave's tail started to wag, "Yeah, what he just said."

Both Retrievers looked at Eddie and Jane pensively for a second, then together they showed big puppy dog eyes.

Eddie said, "OK. Your second hypothesis worked. Congratulations. Tomorrow is an individual training day. Come by the bridge tomorrow morning, I have an idea for an assignment."

Eddie and Jane left the lab and the interns crowded around the two Retrievers to shake their paws and pat them on their backs.

CHAPTER 23

Eddie and Jane left the lab and entered the hallway. Hallway ceilings were lower than lab ceilings. Tommy, a giraffe named after Professor Thomas Odhiambo, a scientist from Kenya, and Chi, a Mandarin duck, named after Chiaki Mukai, the first Japanese woman in space, were coming down the hall. Tommy kept his head down while he walked.

Eddie said, "Hello Chi, hello Tommy."

Tommy heard Eddie, and being polite, knew to look at the person he was talking with. He raised his head and everyone heard a loud metal clang.

Tommy said, "Hello Eddie. Hello Jane."

Jane winced, "That had to hurt. You have to duck when you're up here."

Chi turned to Giraffe and said, "Why do they say duck? We don't lower our heads. Ostriches lower their heads. They should say 'You have to ostrich!' "

Tommy felt the knobs on his head, "I'm OK. Although, I think my ossicones are getting calluses up here. See you later."

Eddie and Jane walked back to the bridge.

CHAPTER 24

The interns sat around the dinner table in the cafeteria and talked about that day's lessons.

"I liked all the examples that Jane mentioned about engineers having an eye for design," said Lu Lu.

"Me too," said Marcos. "That might be a good topic for a research paper."

Everyone nodded.

"Why do you suppose that we see things as attractive versus unattractive?" pondered Thebe.

Jane had wandered by and was listening to their conversation.

"May I join in?" asked Jane.

"Of course," said Liz.

"I think we accept things as attractive because it is the opposite of what we find harmful. For example we like smooth rounded objects, such as an apple, or the smooth lines of a car, or the smooth rounded lines of a Fernando Botero sculpture. They are the opposite of the harmful sharp tooth of a saber tooth tiger. We like soft neutral colors, I'd guess most houses are painted some version of beige, because they are the opposite of a harmful red fire. We accept things that smell good because they are the opposite of food that has gone bad and if eaten would kill us. These concepts, after hundreds of thousands of years of trial and error, are now built in. We accept them."

"So that's why people find me attractive," said Thebe as he stood up and flexed his muscles. "Because I'm rounded and have a soft neutral color."

"You're a pygmy hippo," said Marcos.

"So?" retorted Thebe.

"I bathe with banana scented shampoo. You bathe in mud."

"Well, I'll let you continue that conversation on your own. I have to be on the bridge," said Jane, and walked away quickly.

She could hear Thebe responding, "But the mud has a fresh, outdoorsy smell."

Trying to change the subject, Liz said, "I'm done. I'd like to be a little less rounded, so let's head to the gym."

Everyone agreed and they headed out.

CHAPTER 25

All the interns had a big dinner and a big night at the gym, so they all went to sleep early. Everyone except Marcos. He stayed up just a little later and, now that he knew how to spacewalk, took a little late-night spacewalk. He had figured out a way to get even with Thebe. He took a 3D printout that he made earlier and some duct tape with him. He taped the 3D printout to the outside of Thebe's window next to his bed, returned inside, and went to sleep.

The next morning, Thebe woke up, yawned, and stretched. He rubbed his eyes and looked out his window to see the face of a hideous alien monster staring right at him. He screamed and ran out into the hallway where he stopped to catch his breath.

Eddie heard the scream and ran out of his room and into the hallway. He saw Thebe and went over to him. "What's wrong?"

"Look," Thebe said as he pointed at the angry alien snarling outside his window.

"That's a pretty good 3D printout of an alien," comforted Eddie.

"Oh… I thought it was real. I was really scared," admitted Thebe.

"It could have been."

"You mean you think there really are aliens?"

"I'd be surprised if there weren't. And I'd be disappointed. We've been searching for aliens for a long time. SETI, the Search for Extraterrestrial Intelligence, was started in 1957 to search for alien radio signals."

"We haven't found any yet. Why do you still think there could be aliens?"

"In our universe, we think there are over 100 billion galaxies."

"How do we know that?" Thebe interrupted.

"We can't count every one. We point our telescopes at one part of the universe, say one degree out of 360 degrees, then count as best we can in that area, then multiply by 360."

"Is that accurate?"

"Let's say you are asked to figure out how many apples to buy for the local apple pie festival, but you don't have time to visit all one hundred houses in the neighborhood. You go to the first few houses and find how many people live in each house. Let's say on average there are probably four per house. Then you multiply four times one hundred and you need enough apples to make enough pies to feed four hundred people."

"What if some people don't go to the festival?"

"Some people might not go, some might bring friends or relatives. Close enough."

"OK, I get it."

"All right, so each galaxy has over 100 billion stars. And each star might have say, ten planets. Some planets may be too far away from their sun, and thus too cold for life. Some planets may be too close to their sun and thus too hot for life. Some planets may be in the middle and thus just right for life. We call this the Goldilocks zone. And, like our solar system, there could be one or two."

"You mean one, like Earth."

"Remember, Mars used to have water on its surface. It could have had life wandering around a billion years ago, before life on Earth even started. But let's just say one. That's still 100 hundred billion times 100 billion. How many planets is that?"

"I don't have my calculator, so I'm just going to say a lot."

"That's not a bad answer. So what are the chances that, out of trillions of planets, at least one of them, besides us, has life?"

"I'd say a very good chance."

"Also a good answer. So aliens are probably out there. But if they do come here, what are the chances that they would want to peek specifically into your room?"

"Hopefully zero."

"I think that's the correct answer. So, you OK?"

"Yes, thanks."

"See you at breakfast."

CHAPTER 26

After Eddie left, everyone else came out of their bunk room.

Lu Lu looked at Thebe and said, "We're heading to breakfast. You coming?"

"Thebe took a deep breath, "Yes, of course. I was just talking with Eddie about a science thing."

Andy gave Thebe a pat on the back, "Not to worry. I saw the mask, it's pretty realistic. If I had woken up to that, I would have screamed too."

"I don't think I really screamed," said Thebe in a soft voice.

"Yeah, you screamed," said Marcos. "Come on, I'll walk with you to breakfast."

Marcos and Thebe walked together following the others.

"Hey, I'm sorry," said Marcos. "I didn't think it would bother you that much."

"You did that? Why?"

"What do you mean, why? Mr. 'here have a soda' before my spacewalk."

"Oh, yeah. Sorry." He paused for a moment, "But that was pretty funny."

"You weren't stuck with soda toots in your space suit for an hour."

Thebe nodded.

"Next time we should team up," suggested Marcos.

"What do you mean next time?"

"We're at the cafeteria. We'll talk later."

They walked in and joined the others for breakfast.

CHAPTER 27

During breakfast, John asked, "Hey, where's Dave and Paul?"

"Eddie wanted them to meet him on the bridge this morning," said Lu Lu.

"Maybe they're doing something interesting on our independent study day," suggested Andy.

"Let's go take a look," said Thebe.

They walked to the bridge but didn't see the Retrievers.

"Look outside," said Marcos.

Dave and Paul were outside in their space suits trying to gather up all the tools and other items they had pushed out into space during yesterday's lab experiment. Everyone watched as they retrieved a wrench, then a hammer.

"This will take all day," said Thebe, "I'm going to the gym."

"I'm heading to the lab," said Marcos.

"I'll be in the library," said Lu Lu.

John turned to Chris and Berty, "Call me if they need help with the piano."

Andy and Liz looked out of the front windows, past the Retrievers, at the spinning Earth below. They saw the beginnings of a hurricane forming in the Atlantic Ocean.

"We're going to hang here for a while," Andy said.

"It's odd that spinning white clouds, so beautiful from up here, can be so destructive down there," said Liz.

"This looks like the spin art I did at the beach when I was younger. It was really fun," said Andy.

"I did that too. It was fun."

They continued to watch the progress of the storm.

"Speaking of art, did you ever study the artist Christo in art class?" asked Liz.

"No. Who's he?"

"He did what they call 'land art' or 'environmental art.' "

"What's that?"

"If I remember right, it involves putting up something on the land or on a building for everyone to see, and then, after a while, the artist would take it down. The claim was that it would serve two purposes, one, to be attractive, and two, to make people think."

"What did Christo do?"

"He's most famous for what they called the 'Running Fence' in California. It was six meters high and made out of white nylon fabric. It billowed in the breeze and looked beautiful, but it was only up for 14 days."

"Sounds nice. But why the big deal?"

"Oh sorry, it was 39 kilometers long," said Liz

"Wow."

"Exactly"

"How wide is the hurricane down there?

"I don't know about this one, but on average they're about 600 kilometers wide."

"We could do art bigger than Christo's," said Andy.

"How so?"

"Hurricane spin art."

Liz paused, then smiled, "I like the idea. How would this work?"

"We use drones to drop water balloons filled with paint over the hurricane. We call it 'Extreme Spin Art.' We take a picture and then in a few hours it disappears."

"Cool. But wouldn't the water-based paint just be absorbed right away into the water in the hurricane?"

"Then we use oil-based paint."

"Remember in Earth Science class we learned that one liter of old motor oil can contaminate one million liters of ground water?"

"We're lucky no one dumps old oil down the sewer anymore," said Andy. "Wouldn't the oil-based paint that we dropped into the hurricane also hurt the environment? Wait a minute, we could use vegetable oil mixed with food coloring."

"Good call. And since we probably don't have any water balloons up here, we can use the bio-degradable plastic sanitary food service gloves from the cafeteria, they're pretty thin."

"How many drones will we need?" asked Liz.

"A lot. We'll have to calculate the size of the area on top of the hurricane, then calculate how many balloons it will take to cover that area, and that will determine how many drones we'll need."

"How many do we have up here?"

"Not enough," answered Andy.

"Instead of going to the gym tonight, let's all go to the 3D Printer room and make some drones."

"And get some gloves, vegetable oil, and food coloring from the kitchen."

"Do you think the others will join in?" asked Liz.

"They'll love it. What could go wrong?"

CHAPTER 28

During dinner, Liz and Andy described their plan to the rest of the interns. They all loved the idea and eagerly decided to skip the gym and start working on their new 'Extreme Spin Art' project.

The interns walked quickly from the dining hall to the 3D printer room. They gathered all the plastic filament and started cranking out small drones. These drones were slightly different from regular drones, in that they didn't use propellers, which would be useless in space. Instead, they used mini jet stabilizers, the same mini-jets Eddie used on the spacewalk jetpacks. Once they finished making the drones they gathered all the vegetable oil and food coloring from the kitchen. They mixed the two ingredients together in the large food mixing bowls and made paints of every color. Next they used large mixing spoons to fill the plastic gloves with paint and tied a knot in the gloves to keep the paint from spilling out. They attached the paint balloons to pincer hooks on the bottom of the drones. The final step was to carry all the drones to the airlock bays. This took several trips as they had made 90 paint balloon drones. They had worked all night and it was early enough that no one else was in the hallways. They opened all the inner airlock doors and placed the drones inside the airlocks. They closed the inner doors. John, and Dave and Paul stayed at the airlocks while the rest hurried to the bridge.

When the interns arrived on the bridge there were just a few members of the night crew manning the controls. They were used to the comings and goings of the interns and so didn't think anything was out of the ordinary. The interns made their way to the main windows. The timing was perfect, daylight was just breaking over the Atlantic Ocean and, just as the weather models predicted, a small hurricane was forming.

Liz whispered into her phone, "Hello John. Are you there?"

"Yes," whispered John into his phone.

"Release the drones," said Liz, still whispering.

John, Dave, and Paul pressed the buttons and three outer airlock doors opened.

"Outer doors open," said John.

Andy started to move the joystick on the control box. They made all the drones use the same frequency so they could all be maneuvered simultaneously. All ninety drones hovered out of the airlock bays. John, Dave, and Paul pressed the buttons to close the outer doors and then walked quickly to the bridge. They arrived on the bridge in time to see the last of the drones fade from view as they hovered down toward the hurricane.

After a few minutes, the interns could see the hurricane coming into view on the control box screen as a few of the drones had been fitted with cameras. The drones got closer and closer.

Andy looked at the others and they all nodded. It was time. Andy pushed a button on the control box.

Liz said, "I hope the pincers let loose of the paint balloons."

They all leaned into the windows a little more.

"Look, look," said Lu Lu and pointed.

It was working. First a little swirl, then more, then the entire top of the hurricane was swirling in a rainbow of colors.

"Awesome," said Andy, as he high-fived Liz.

All the interns were cheering.

"Beautiful actually," said Eddie.

"Christo would be proud," said Jane.

The interns were stunned, their eyes grew wide and they turned around.

Eddie pointed to the big screen which by now was showing close-ups of the hurricane via the high resolution cameras on the Space Zoo 1.

John whispered to the group, "Are they smiling?"

"It appears so," whispered Lu Lu.

"Don't forget to retrieve the drones," said Eddie.

Andy quickly looked down at the control box and steered the drones back to the airlock bays.

"I'll go open the outer doors," said John.

"How long have you been watching?" asked Andy.

"Since last night," said Jane. "There are motion sensors and cameras in all the labs, airlocks, and main rooms of Space Zoo 1, just in case anything goes wrong."

"Jane called me and said 'You have to see this.' We met in the Captain's Lounge, made some hot tea, and stayed up all night watching your progress."

"If anything went wrong we would have stepped in," said Jane.

"To stop us?" asked Liz.

"No," said Eddie, "to help. This was an amazing project. You have used all your skills. We are proud of your initiative."

The interns all smiled. John returned and was happy to see everyone smiling.

"Of course we'll have to order a replacement shipment of printer filament, gloves, vegetable oil, and food dye," said Eddie.

Chris was in his chair when a call came in. Chris turned in his chair and looked at Eddie, "Captain, you have a call coming in from the International Hurricane Center."

"Put it on speaker, please. They're probably calling to tell us how impressed they are with your environmental art."
The speaker crackled, "Captain, this is Dr. Eyewall, Director of the International Hurricane Center in Florida."
"Hello, Director. What can we do for you?"
"We sent a research airplane into the newly forming hurricane to get air speed measurements. It used to be silver. Now it's a blue-green color. Any idea how that happened?"
Jane pushed some buttons on her computer. On the big screen they could see the camera zoom in from the top of the hurricane to show the plane as it was flying out of the hurricane. It was covered in paint.
"Yes, we have an idea of how that happened. Sorry. We'll send down a crew to clean the plane up," said Eddie.
"Thank you," said the Director, and he hung up.
"I know you all are tired, but I think we need to fix this right away. Have a Zoomerang take you down, clean it up, and spend the day sleeping on the beach."
The interns, tried to keep from snickering. They left the bridge to go move all the returned drones back into the printer room before their departure.
Eddie leaned over to Jane, "I thought the plane was more of a greenish-blue."
Jane smiled, "No, he was right, it was a blue-green."
They continued to watch the hurricane out of the main windows.
"Definitely greenish-blue."
"No," repeated Jane. "Blue-green."

CHAPTER 29

The interns took the next Zoomerang down to Florida and spent a couple of hours with sponges and hoses cleaning off of the research airplane. Then Dr. Eyewall gave them a tour of the International Hurricane Center facility. Afterwards, in the van on the way to the beach they all talked about how they were going to swim, surf, and snorkel. As soon as they got onto the warm sand and put down their towels, each one of them promptly fell asleep for a much needed rest.

When the interns returned to Space Zoo 1, they reported to Eddie and Jane on the bridge.

"We met with Dr. Eyewall and took a tour of their facility," said Andy.

"They do very interesting work there. We saw the rest of the airplanes, the satellite center, and all the computers," added John.

"We learned how destructive hurricanes are, and saw pictures of kilometers and kilometers of houses and trees completely flattened," said Lu Lu.

"There have been thousands of deaths over the last hundred years," said Marcos, "although with today's early warning satellites, the number of deaths recently has dropped way down."

"Also, the property destruction has been in the hundreds of billions of dollars," said Thebe.

"We're glad you went. Sounds like it was a worthwhile field trip," said Jane.

"It gave us an idea," said Liz. "And when we went to the beach we asked the Zoomerang pilot to do a little shopping for us."

"Oh good. I love toffee from the beach," said Eddie.

Jane winced at Eddie and shook her head.

"What?" asked Eddie.

"We got water pumps, tubing, and wire mesh from the hardware store," said Thebe.

"You guys really know how to have a good time," said Chris, who had been listening in on the conversation. He looked at Eddie and Jane and said, "Next time you have to send them to Florida, send them during Spring Break."

"When we migrate, it's not to get out of the cold, we just like the Spring Break party scene," said Berty.

"We're heading to the labs. We're rested and ready to get to work," said Andy.

As they turned to leave, Marcos looked at Eddie and Jane and said, "The Zoomerang pilot said he would be sending you the bill. Is that OK?"

"That's OK. Next time add a box of toffee," smiled Eddie.

The interns got to work in the lab. Over the next several days, they made even more drones. They made scoops out of the wire mesh, which they attached to one-third of the drones. They hooked the water pumps to the tubing, which they attached to one-third of the drones. And they filled another batch of plastic gloves with vegetable oil and hooked those gloves to the original drones with the pincers. Then they walked slowly back to their bunks and fell fast asleep.

Several hours later, there was a loud honk and a knock on the door. The interns jumped out of their beds and Marcos was first to the door. He opened it and there was Chris.

"You guys asked me to come wake you at the first sign of a new hurricane."

"Yes, thanks. We didn't know it would be so soon," said Marcos sleepily.

"It's hurricane season," said Chris. "I understand you have a new project you all have been working on."

"Yep, we'll be down to the bridge in a few minutes."

Everyone hustled to the lab and then hauled every drone to the air locks. This time it took several more trips. Thebe, John, and Lu Lu stayed to work the airlock doors. The rest ran to the bridge.

They went through the same procedures as before and close to three hundred drones hovered out of the airlocks.

The word had spread and this time almost the entire Space Zoo Patrol team was waiting on the bridge. They cleared a path so the airlock crew could make their way to the front by the main window.

Andy cleared his throat and announced, "The hurricane is just forming and it is small. We figured now is the time to try to destabilize it before it grows into a destructive force."

Everyone watched as the swarm of drones hovered down out of sight. The drone cameras then turned on and their video stream came on the big screen. Everyone turned their attention to the big screen.

The drones hovered right past the swirling top and swooped down to ocean level.

Andy had one control box and he steered one group of drones into the path in front of the hurricane. He pushed a button on the box and all the oil balloons dropped into the path where the material formed a huge slick.

Andy said, "This vegetable oil slick will form a barrier and keep the hurricane from absorbing the heat from the surface of the ocean so the hurricane can't gain strength."

There was some mild applause from the crowd.

Marcos had another control box and he steered his drones directly behind the hurricane. They hovered just above the waves and Marcos pushed a button on his box which sent a signal to let down the hoses. Once the hoses were all down, Marcos pushed another button and the pumps turned on.

Marcos said to the crowd, "The pumps are bringing up cold water from below the surface and the hoses are spraying the cold water into the hurricane, really making sure there is no heat energy in the hurricane."

The applause grew a little louder.

Liz had the third box and steered her drones back and forth on the ocean to the side of the hurricane. They were using the wire mesh scoops to scoop up tons of seaweed. "The seaweed is being sprayed with hot gelatin, one of the main ingredients of molded jelly desserts. When the hot gelatin hits the cold seaweed, it gels together."

Liz continued, "Let me know when you think the hurricane is starting to weaken."

Everyone watched closely. It looked for a second as if it was weakening and everyone was leaning forward and about to shout, but the hurricane started to look thicker. Then for a second it looked as if it was thinning just a bit. Everyone started shouting, "Now! Now!"

Liz pushed the button on her control box and all the drones dumped the seaweed on one side of the hurricane. They could all see a massive lump on one side of the hurricane which kept spinning around and made the hurricane wobble like a spinning top about to fall over. The hurricane wobbled off to the left.

Everyone on the bridge leaned over a little to the left, as if helping the hurricane, and they all were saying slowly, "Whoooa!" And "Tip, tip, tip!"

Then the hurricane wobbled to the right. Everyone leaned a little to the right and said "Go, go, go!" And "Come on, tip over!"

Then it wobbled backward until it finally fell over. And the hurricane was gone.

Everyone erupted into wild applause. The interns couldn't help but grin. They looked over at Jane and Eddie. It was hard to tell who was grinning more, the interns or Jane and Eddie.

CHAPTER 30

Marcos had already taken his introductory spacewalk, now it was Liz's turn. Eddie and Liz suited up in their spacesuits and stood at one of the airlocks.

Jane happened to walk by and said to Eddie, "Good morning, Eddie. Good morning, Liz. What's happening here?"

"Good morning, Jane," said Eddie. "We're just getting prepared to go outside for Liz's first spacewalk."

"Have fun, Liz. You are in good paws. Eddie designed our space suits. He's our best engineer. The old original space suits were heavy, bulky, and difficult to maneuver in. The new suits used newer materials, such as spandex and nylon, and are trimmer and easier to maneuver in. Eddie knows what he's doing out there."

"Yes, Sir," responded Liz.

Jane looked closely into Liz's visor. "Is that a smirk?"

"No, Sir," stammered Liz.

Jane looked at Liz.

Liz looked at Eddie. "I'm sorry sir. I'll change my screensaver," she said in a soft voice.

"It's no problem," said Eddie.

"All right," said Jane. "You be careful out there." She turned to walk away, but stopped and turned back. "But have fun." She turned and walked out to the hallway, where they heard her say, "But be careful."

"Are you ready to go have some fun?" asked Eddie.

"Yes," replied Liz.

They stepped into the airlock, and closed the inner door. They turned around and faced the outer door which Eddie then opened.

"Just like in training, use the joystick to move out of the airlock."

They both eased out slowly.

"How do you like the fit of your EVA suit?" asked Eddie.

Liz stared straight ahead and whispered, "My what?"

"Your extra vehicular activity spacesuit. Remember extra means external or outside of? It's one of the terms you were supposed to have studied."

"I studied. I'm a little nervous."

"Why, because you're floating in space?"

"No. Because we're floating 400 kilometers above the Earth."

"Oh, you looked down."

"Yes."

"Don't look down."

"Too late."

"You're experiencing vertigo. Not to worry, everyone gets it at first. Vertigo is when you feel dizzy or faint from looking down from someplace high. Most people feel it when they look down from a tall building or cliff, then they instinctively step back from the edge and the feeling goes away. It's a built-in biological safety feature that has evolved over time to keep us safe. OK, let's walk you through this. Take a deep breath."

Liz took a deep breath.

"Look at me."

Liz looked at Eddie.

"Now look past me at the stars."

"They're not twinkling."

"We're in space. There's no atmosphere to refract or distort the stars' light."

Liz stared at Eddie.

"You knew that."

Liz nodded, "Thanks though."

'*The small talk is working, she's calming down,*' thought Eddie, '*time to move to the next phase.*'

"Turn your head and look at Space Zoo 1. That's your new reference point."

Liz looked at the huge space station.

"Now look down at Earth for one second, then back at me."

Liz did so.

"What did you see?"

"A spinning Earth."

"How fast is it spinning?"

"1670 kilometers per hour."

"Look again for two seconds."

This time Liz looked for two seconds.

"What did you see?"

"The Atlantic Ocean."

"How about now?"

Liz looked down for five or six seconds, "Here comes North America and South America."

"How are you feeling now?"

"Better, thanks."

"Once you get the hang of it, you could watch for hours at a time."

"Next time, right now I should probably get back to my spacewalk initiation checklist."

They went through the same set of spacewalk routines that Eddie had performed earlier when he was testing his new jetpack, and with Marcos: forward, backward, spin, etc.

"That went well," said Eddie.

"Thanks."

"Why don't we just sit a spell and watch the world go by?"

"Sounds good to me."

They watched contentedly as the Earth rotated below them, pointing out land formations and weather patterns.

After a few minutes, Liz asked, "We're not really sitting are we?"

"No, that's just an expression. I come from mountain folk."

"Good. I just wanted to be sure that wasn't some technical term that I hadn't studied."

Eddie smiled.

After a few more minutes, they headed back inside. Over the next few days, the other interns completed their introductory spacewalks as well.

Space Zoo Patrol

CHAPTER 31

The next day Marcos went to the bridge. He looked around but didn't see Eddie, so he went over to Jane who was looking at a computer screen.

"Hi, Jane, excuse me."

"Hello, Marcos. How can I help you?"

"I am looking for Eddie. I want to thank him for helping me get through my spacewalk."

"He'll appreciate that. He's in his lab."

"What's he working on?"

"He won't say. That probably means he wants to be left alone"

"OK, thanks. I'll come back later."

He turned and walked off the bridge. As he walked down the hall he thought to himself, '*I should just go see Eddie. On the one hand, it's good etiquette to thank someone as soon as you can after they have given you something or helped you. On the other hand, Jane said he wanted to be left alone. On the other-other hand, the fact that he is in the lab and is working on something secretive sounds interesting.*' So he did what any curious intern would do, he took the elevator down to the lab level, went to Eddie's personal lab, Lab 51, and knocked.

"Who's there?" came Eddie's voice from the other side of the door.

"Ivana," said Marcos, who snickered under his breath. Eddie was puzzled as he didn't know any Ivana aboard the Space Zoo 1. "Ivana who?"

"Ivana come see your experiment," responded Marcos. Eddie appreciated a good sense of humor, and knew it was related to intelligence. He now recognized the voice and said, "Come on in." He pushed a button under the lab workbench to unlock the door.

Marcos heard the door unlock, opened the door, and walked in.

"Hi, Marcos. How can I help you?"

"Hello, Sir. I just thought I'd stop by and say thanks for helping me through my spacewalk. I loved it."

"Glad it went well."

Marcos looked around the lab, "Also, I wanted to see what you are working on."

Eddie proudly held up his new invention, "Jet boots."

"What are they for?"

"Primarily to get you out of emergencies. Such as quicksand. Or if you're getting a lava sample and the crust starts to break through. Or if you need to cross a stream quickly. You slip them over your existing boots and you can still walk normally."

"Sounds helpful. They look like they're finished."

"All except for a trial run."

"I can spot you, if you'd like."

"Usually Jane helps with that. But sure, let's go ahead."

Eddie slipped on the jet boots. "I thought about these boots some time ago, and I've already programmed the wrist control panel on all of our spacesuits to allow us to activate the boots." He pushed some buttons on his wrist and hovered up slowly. He smiled.

Marcos gave a thumbs up.

Then Eddie wobbled a bit, then the boots kicked into full thrust. Eddie flew sideways and smacked into the wall.

"Sorry, I didn't catch you. That happened so fast," said Marcos. "Are you OK?"

"Accidents happen very quickly. That's why I should have thought of what might have happened and then created a harness system to use during trial runs. Oh well. I think I just need to add gyroscopic stabilizers." Eddie got up and dusted himself off. "But first, let's go get lunch. I've been working all morning and missed breakfast." Eddie slipped off his jet boots.

As they headed out, Eddie added, "Just no pictures, no screen savers."

"Your secret is safe with me," smiled Marcos

CHAPTER 32

Chris was on the bridge checking the e-mails coming in from Earth, when one e-mail in particular seemed urgent. It just read: 'please hurry…please see attachment.' He looked at the attachment, said aloud "Oh my goodness." He pushed the intercom button and said in as calm a voice as he could muster, "Eddie, Jane, please come to the bridge." Moments later Eddie and Jane arrived on the bridge and Jane said, "Chris, what is it?"

"We got an e-mail from the U.S. saying 'please hurry' and there's an attachment, take a look."

The attachment was a video. They saw a shaky picture, obviously taken from a helmet cam. The voice said "Here's our family's empty crick shed." Then some shaky footage as the helmet cam went to the next house and showed another empty crick shed. This repeated for a third shed. As the video swayed side to side they could see that there were several kids on bikes, all with helmets and helmet cams. One of the kids took off his helmet cam and turned it back to face himself and his friends.

"Space Zoo Patrol, please help us. This is the tenth storage shed in our neighborhood that has been cleaned out of all the crickets we've been collecting for months. Food is getting scarce and expensive. Our parents are too busy working and the police said this is happening everywhere, but there is no law against stealing crickets. Thanks. Your pals from Shepardville."

Jane looked at Eddie, "Well, we've known for some time that food has been getting scarcer on Earth. Now it appears things have taken a turn for the worse. We need to work on this."

"Agreed," said Eddie. He then leaned over his microphone, "All interns please meet at the conference room now."

CHAPTER 33

A few minutes later, Eddie, Jane, and the interns all assembled in the conference room.

Eddie and Jane, as usual, stood at the front of the room. The interns quickly sat down and didn't say a word. They saw that Eddie and Jane looked serious.

Jane spoke first, "We just received a troubling e-mail. It was a call to action, a wake-up call."

Eddie said, "We've been notified that someone is stealing food. The message came from one small town. But we think the problem is much more widespread. There have been food shortages over the centuries. Occasionally from natural causes like drought or crop failure. Sometimes during wars. Sometimes people just live in places where it's hard to grow food. Even today, there are several hundred million people who do not have enough food to lead a healthy life. Imagine, if they all had a proper food supply they could concentrate on having a happy, healthy, productive life. Having a safe, secure, sustainable food supply should be the top priority of all societies. Frankly, I am a little embarrassed that it has gotten this bad and we haven't done anything about it yet."

"Why hasn't anyone back on Earth done anything about it?" asked Marcos.

"There are plenty of good people working on this," said Jane. "However, there are lots of other priorities that pop up as well, such as developing new medicines, paving roads, building libraries, cleaning up after storms. The list is endless. And occasionally we even have to sleep."

The interns smiled.

Eddie continued, "And occasionally we have to step back and relax for a bit, or the stress of the continuous demands of trying to move society forward would become too hard to bear. So, people who juggle or tell jokes or make movies are essential too. Everyone is busy doing their jobs and getting on with their lives. So sometimes, something important comes along and we don't notice it."

"We think it's time to notice the food problem," Jane said solemnly.

Eddie thumped his tail several times, and said with a clear steady voice, "So what do you think? Should the Space Zoo Patrol step up to the plate and tackle this problem?"

The interns pounded the table with their fists and yelled, "Yeah."

"All right. Let's go to my lab. I have a few ideas to get us started," said Eddie.

As they were walking out, Jane leaned over to Eddie and whispered, "You mixed your metaphors again."

"I know. I'm sorry. I was excited."

CHAPTER 34

Eddie, Jane, and the interns all assembled in Eddie's Lab 51.

"We are going to have to put aside our research in other areas and put all our efforts into finding more food," said Eddie.

Everyone leaned in and look at him attentively.

Eddie stopped, thought for a minute, then said, "We're going to need a four-prong approach."

He raised one finger in the air, for emphasis, "First, let's keep the food we've got. I understand a lot of food goes to waste. Interns, I want some of you to research the best ways on how to keep food from going bad."

Some of the interns started nodding their heads indicating they liked that research assignment.

Eddie raised two fingers, "Second, let's figure out how to grow more food down on the planet."

The interns that had not been nodding at the first one were nodding at this one.

Eddie raised three fingers, "Third, we're also going to have to look elsewhere for food. So, we'll speed up the search for exoplanets."

Everyone looked surprised.

"Jane, you know the Very Large Array telescope organizations. You can contact them."

Jane asked, "How many?"

Eddie looked directly at Jane and said seriously, "All of them."

Jane looked at the interns, "We will be looking for what is called an exoplanet, a planet outside of our solar system. Exo meaning outside of, like a bug has an exoskeleton, a skeleton outside of its body."

"Will they be difficult to find?" asked Andy.

"We have been looking for exoplanets for some time now," continued Jane. "The first planet outside of our solar system was found in 1992. By 2015, astronomers had discovered over one thousand. Since then we have found over one hundred thousand."

Jane looked at Eddie and said, "Happy to do that." Then looked back at the interns and said, "We need HELP."

"We know," said Lu Lu. "We'll give you all the help you need."

"Thank you. I meant H.E.L.P. Habitable Earth Like Planets."

"What's that?" asked John.

"For a planet to be helpful to us, it will have to be similar to our planet. It has to be the right composition, it has to be solid like Earth, not a gas giant like Saturn. It has to be the right temperature, so it must be the right distance from its sun like Earth. Not too far away or it will be an ice ball like Pluto, not too close or it will be too hot like Mercury which is over 400 degrees Celsius. It has to have a magnetic field so it can fend off solar rays and keep an atmosphere, although there is a debate about that. And of course it has to have water. There are exoplanets of every description. We will be searching specifically for exoplanets with just the requirements that I listed."

Jane turned her head from side to side for a few moments, then said, "We're gonna need a bigger telescope."

Eddie looked at Jane and said, "What do you mean?"

"We will need the combination of all of our telescopes to determine these requirements. So far, we have only examined space by using each telescope separately. If we really want to start exploring, we're going to have to synchronize, or synch, them altogether to form one big telescope."

"That's never been done before," said Eddie.

"Well, we have a serious problem and so it's time to get serious about the solution."

"Which telescopes are you talking about?"

"All of them, the radio telescopes, the optical telescopes, the infrared telescopes, and the high-energy telescopes."

"The land-based and the space-based?"

"All of them."

"How do you synch them?" asked Marcos.

"We'll combine their inputs into multiple super biocomputers to form one very big, very detailed picture."

"Sort of like combining pixels in a TV monitor to make one big picture," said Andy.

"Exactly."

"Sort of like painting lots of small dots to make a pointillism painting," added Liz.

"Yes."

"Sort of like gathering every grain of sand to make a beach," added Thebe.

"Yes, yes, that works too. I think you all get it."

"I'm curious. When was the first telescope invented?" asked Lu Lu.

"Our eyes were the first telescopes," replied Jane. "Using our naked eyes..."

The interns snickered.

Eddie looked cross. "That's the term. Naked eyes."

They snickered again.

Jane took over, "OK. Using our '*un-aided*' eyes, we can see the moon, the sun, Mercury, Venus, Mars, Jupiter, and Saturn. But we are a curious lot and after centuries of looking up we tried to figure out how to see more. The story is that, in 1608, a Dutch maker of eyeglasses saw some inquisitive children in his shop holding up two eye glass pieces so that they could make things on the other side of the shop look closer. He fitted the two pieces into a tube to hold them steady and made the first telescope. The Dutch government paid him to make many more, and astronomy was born."

"So, specifically which telescopes should you call first?" asked Eddie.

Jane said, "OK. I'll start with the space-based Spitzer, Kepler, and Hubble, then call the land-based Giant Magellan in Chile, the Thirty Meter in Hawaii, the EELT in Chile, and Keck One and Two in Hawaii. If we get those, the other smaller ones will join in."

Eddie looked upset, "Combining that many telescopes together has never been done before. That's going to take a lot of computer power to synch them up."

Jane smiled, "I will also call every organization with super computers, the Pentagon, NASA, the National Oceanographic and Atmospheric Administration, and every engineering university in the United States."

Eddie looked at the interns and said, "There's a lot to get done. We have our assignments. We better get to work."

Everyone turned to leave.

"Wait, wait," said Thebe.

Everyone stopped and looked back.

Thebe said, "What's the fourth prong?"

Eddie smiled, "Good catch. The fourth prong is," and he paused for emphasis, "let's catch the creeps who've been stealing the cricks."

Everyone cheered.

Eddie said, "I'll get Chris to send the kids in Shepardville several tracker launchers. We'll figure out a way to lure the creeps back, and zap whatever they're driving with the tracking beacons. We'll track it from here and figure out who is stealing the cricks." Eddie paused for a second, "Actually, there is a fifth prong. I have an idea that will require that I spend the next few days uninterrupted in my lab." Eddie started to look around the lab, taking a mental note of things he would need.

Jane looked at the interns, lifted her wing, and pointed to the door. Everyone quietly exited out into the hallway. Once they got in the hallway and the lab door was closed, they immediately started excitedly talking about what they thought Eddie was doing.

Jane popped back into the lab, "You didn't tell me what you're going to do. I suspect you've thought of a way to get to whatever exoplanet we find."

"They don't call you a wise old owl for nothing."

"Who calls me old?"

"Nobody, it's just an expression."

"You don't see any gray feathers on me. Do you?"

"I thought all owls had gray feathers. I mean except you. Yours are mostly brown. I mean all brown." Eddie paused, he felt he wasn't saying the right things. "You look great. Can I please start building a spaceship?"

"Not to worry. It takes a lot more than that to ruffle my feathers. And I wouldn't worry about that little patch of gray fur on the back of your head." Jane slipped out of the lab.

Eddie started looking at various piles of parts ad tools around the lab. Then he looked up, walked over to the mirror, and started trying to look for any gray on the back of his head. "No way. She has to be joking," he said aloud. Eddie picked up a notepad and pen and went back to poking around the lab, making notes as to what he needed.

After a minute, he went back to the mirror for a second look. He said to the mirror, "Nothing. And why would I care anyway, even if there was some gray. Which there's not."

CHAPTER 35

Glenn's parent's house was small but well-maintained in a nice suburban neighborhood. The doorbell rang, Glenn's mom stopped making lunch, and answered the front door. Her mouth hung open and her eyes opened wide as she stared at a small yellow drone, which hovered at eye-level. The drone spoke in a soft but metallic sounding voice, "Is Glenn home? He has a package."
Mom continued to stare straight ahead at the drone but turned her mouth sideways. She didn't yell but slightly raised her voice, "Glenn… you have a package."

For years, it had been pretty common to order most things from the Internet and get the item delivered. Many people still went to the malls to socialize, browse, and look at things they ended up buying on-line. Malls realized sales were declining and ended up charging an admission fee, like any other entertainment place. Surprisingly people still went.

Glenn had ordered several things recently and wasn't sure if he should get up from his homework just to sign for a package. He could let his mom sign. His mom could hear his voice as it came from his bedroom, "Post Office?"
"No."
"Fed Ex?"
"No."
She continued to stare straight ahead.
"UPS?"
"No."
"Who is it from?"

His mom leaned sideways just a little to look past the small hovering drone and saw a much larger drone, also yellow, hovering in the front yard. She read the lettering on the side and called back to Glenn, "Space Zoo Patrol."

Glenn was at the front door in about a second, "I'm Glenn." The small drone turned around and went back to the large drone where there was an opening in the side. The small drone picked out a package with its mechanical claws and brought the package to the front door. It handed the package to Glenn who said, "Thank you."

The drone responded, "Good luck." It turned around and went back inside the side opening of the larger drone. The side door closed and the large drone quickly hovered away. As Glenn started to run upstairs, his mom called after him, "What did it mean by good luck?"

All she heard was, "Later, Mom."

Glenn went into his room and opened the package. It contained a sheet of paper with a list of instructions and four tracker launchers. He shouted to his sister, and immediately texted his friends, 'Come on over. Hurry.'

Glenn and Sally waited for them downstairs. After a few minutes they arrived and they all went upstairs to his room. They sat or stood and didn't say a word. They saw the SZP logo on the package.

Glenn held up the sheet of paper and said, "We have some instructions." Then he read aloud, "Number one - Find a place to build a big crick storage pantry next to a street."

Sally said, "That's easy, the entrance to the park a block from here."

Everyone nodded.

"Number two - Find some spare wood and build a pantry."

Kali said, "My dad has a lot of leftover plywood."

"We've got a bunch of two-by-fours," said Mario.

Glenn said, "Great! So far so good. Number three - gather as many extra cricks as you can to fill up the pantry. That will be the bait."

Sally said, "If we each go to three or four neighbors we should have enough."

"That'll be easy, they'll all want to help," Mario nodded in agreement.

Glenn continued, "Number four - When you're done, call Janet, the reporter from the local news. We already contacted her. She's agreed to interview you. When you are interviewed, read the attached story. That will announce the bait." Glenn held up the second page.

Kali said, "Wow, we're gonna be on TV."

"Cool," said Mario. "I nominate Glenn as the spokesperson."

"I've never been on TV," protested Glenn.

"None of us have. This was your idea, you deserve the credit," said Sally.

"OK," said Glenn. "Number five - After the interview is on TV, hide-out and watch the pantry. If someone steals the cricks, shoot their vehicle with the tracker launchers." Glenn held up one of the tracker launchers. "The people in the vehicle won't know they've been hit. We'll handle the tracking from here."

Everyone reached in to pick up a tracker launcher.

"One last part," said Glenn. "Number six - Don't get caught."

"Everything sounded easy till the last part," said Sally.

"You're a fast runner," said Glenn. "Remember when you…"

Mario cut him off, "That never happened."

"All right, everyone," said Glenn. "Put the tracker launchers back in the box."

They placed the trackers in the box, which Glenn slid under his bed.

"Shall we start building the shed?" asked Glenn enthusiastically.

"Yeah," said Sally.

"Let's go," said Mario as he pumped his fist.

CHAPTER 36

The next day, the interns were in the cafeteria having lunch and discussing their new research assignments. Jane walked by and Liz said, "Jane, excuse me. Do you have time for a quick question?"

"Of course," said Jane.

"Yesterday, when we first got together to discuss the food crisis, Eddie mentioned that occasionally, something important happens and we don't notice it. We've been discussing that we have all also seen that occasionally something important happens and people do notice it, but still don't do anything."

"How can that be?" asked John.

"Sometimes change doesn't happen because of inertia," responded Jane.

"What does that mean?" asked Thebe.

"Well you know what inertia is," said Jane.

"Yes. Inertia is when something stays the same, whether it is at rest or moving in a straight line," said Thebe.

"Correct. And it will stay that way unless something from the outside changes that inertia. For example, a book will sit, or rest, on a table forever until someone comes and picks it up. Or, an asteroid will continue in a straight line until it is hit by another asteroid or its path is disrupted by the gravity of some planet. Centuries ago, people thought that the Earth was the center of our solar system. And why should they have doubted that? Everything they knew existed here. Then, some very smart people developed telescopes and made some mathematical calculations that showed that our sun is the center of our solar system. More recently, it took decades for American college football to develop a playoff system."

Marcos asked a more specific question, "But why are people reluctant to make changes when something new is obviously the right way or the better way? Why does it take so long to make the change?"

"People get used to doing something a certain way. Maybe they like it that way. For example, you can try many different flavors of ice cream, but your favorite, after many years, is still chocolate. Or, it's easier that way. Or, they aren't sure what will happen if the change is made. All perfectly normal reactions. Or, on the other hand people can be lazy and not care. Or, there is pressure from companies that would go out of business if everyone made a change."

"Such as?" asked Liz.

"The oil, coal, and nuclear industries all tried to stop renewable energy when it first came out.

The train companies tried to stop the automobile companies. They even had a governor write to the President telling him that cars went too fast and scared the horse-drawn carriages.

Later, the largest American auto companies bought out the Los Angeles trolley system and dismantled it so that people were forced to buy cars. Competition is brutal. But a competitive system ensures that consumers get many choices and the best ideas get to the top. Those ideas will survive until the next better idea comes along.

"What can we do to speed things up?" asked Marcos.

"Maybe that's part of our job as scientists, to make something really, really better than the old way. Or, to explain it in such a way that it really, really makes sense to make the change. You can't just invent or discover something, then hide in the lab."

"That helps. Thank you," said Andy.

"Good, happy to help. I must get to the bridge, so see you all later."

As Jane departed, Marcos said, "Chocolate is OK, but the obviously superior ice cream is Banana Blast with chunks of banana."

"Are you kidding?" asked John. "The obvious choice of ice cream is Sardine Supreme with chunks of seaweed."

Everyone stared at John.

"Blame inertia," said Lu Lu. "But it's going to take me a long time to accept that Sardine Supreme is even a flavor."

CHAPTER 37

After five days, the interns had completed their research and Jane had successfully made her calls. The telescope community around the world dropped their regular projects, synched up their telescopes, and fed the results into 135 super biocomputers around the world. They found hundreds of suitable exoplanets. Everyone waited on Eddie.

The next morning Eddie called Jane, "Did you find a planet?"

"Yes. There were hundreds to choose from, but the interns and I liked this one best. By the way, it's 5,000 light years away."

Eddie replied, "No problem."

Jane said, "That's good to hear, because I thought, you know, that a spaceship even traveling at the speed of light would still take 5,000 years to get there, and that might be a problem."

Eddie said, "Nope. I just need the planet's galactic coordinates."

Jane typed into her computer and said, "I'm e-mailing them to you now."

"Got them, thanks. I'll call you later."

Later that evening, Eddie called Jane again, "Come on over to my lab."

"I'll be right there," said Jane. She stood up and said, "Chris and Berty, you have the bridge." She then quickly went down the hallway to Lab 51.

Jane knocked on the door to Eddie's lab and said, "Today's secret word is exoplanet."

Eddie smiled and pushed the button under his lab desk and the door unlocked. Jane walked in.

Eddie took a loud sip from his ginger lemonade then said, "I think everything is completely ready."

Jane nodded and said, "You've triple checked everything?"

"Have a seat," said Eddie as he pushed his lab chair over to Jane. She sat down. Eddie took a few steps backward and pulled at a tarp.

Jane leaned back in the chair and said, "I've got to tell you, this is one beautiful machine."

The spaceship was amazing. A perfect sphere about three meters in diameter that glowed a pale blue.

Eddie proudly stated, "The sphere is made of multiple layers of graphene to protect the passengers. On the inside are all of the mechanical components, including the electrical wiring, computers, and navigation system. Covering the components are a series of removable plastic cabinet doors that keep the passengers from bumping into the components. Sprayed over the outer shell is a semi-sticky clear material, like on a Post-it note. Sprayed onto the sticky coating is a layer of quarks."

"How do you get in?"

"The door is voice activated. I thought a handle on the outside would cause aerodynamic problems." Eddie turned to the spaceship and said, "Door open." The door hissed as it opened. Jane peered in and saw seven seats inside.

Jane just stared, turning her head left then right.

"Who are we going to take on the trip?" asked Eddie.

"What do you mean, we?" asked Jane.

"What do you mean, what do you mean?" retorted Eddie.

"What do you mean, what do you mean, what do you mean?" shot back Jane.

"I asked first," said Eddie.

"I'd love to go, obviously," said Jane. "But you know the regulations – 'Both senior officers can't leave Space Zoo 1 on the same mission.' "

Eddie said, "I know. But that's just for dangerous missions in case we both don't make it back, no one would be here to run things."

Jane looked quizzical, "You don't consider this a dangerous mission?"

Eddie looked straight at her and said, "No."

Jane stared at Eddie.

Eddie continued, "You know, more people are hit by lightning than get hurt by galactic space travel."

Jane stared at Eddie.

Eddie gave a huge grin.

Jane leaned back, "You didn't?"

Eddie kept grinning, "I did."

"You already went?"

"Yes."

"When?"

"This morning after I got the exoplanet's coordinates from you. I quadruple checked everything."

"How long were you gone?'

"I was gone for less than a minute."

Jane stared at Eddie. Jane's jaw dropped.

"I know. Cool huh?" Eddie was still grinning.

"Do you need a lecture on how dangerous that was to leave without telling anyone?"

"I was 5,000 light years out of cell phone range. It's not like I could have called if things went wrong."

"OK. OK. Tell me about the trip."

"I sprayed on the quarks, I jumped into the spaceship, closed the door, set the location gauges with your galactic coordinates, and pushed the launch button." He took a breath and continued, "I felt a very small rocking sensation. Then nothing. I figured nothing had happened. I popped up the periscope and saw that I was in a field with billions of mushrooms and nothing looked dangerous. I did an atmosphere test and, obviously your telescope measurements were on target, the air is fine. So I opened the door and there I was."

Jane's eyes were much bigger than normal.

Eddie continued, "I reached out, grabbed a few mushrooms, closed the door, hit the return button, and poof, back here in a couple of seconds."

Jane let out a little "Whoooo," as a sigh of relief.

"And…" Eddie reached over and pulled a plastic food container from his lab fridge. He opened it and showed it to Jane. The container was filled with mushrooms. They were pink. He handed one to Jane. "Try this."

"Are you sure it's safe? You know you should never eat a mushroom unless you know it's safe."

"Obviously. When I returned, I took them to the bio-lab and tested them."

"What were the results?"

"One hundred percent safe, filled with nutrients, and they taste like…"

Jane took a bite and gave a big smile, "Like strawberries!"

Eddie nodded, "They're delicious."

Jane took another bite. "So, it'll be safe to take the interns?"

"Yes. But I need a good night's sleep. We'll give them a briefing in the morning."

CHAPTER 38

Eddie had worked hard for the last six days and had been exhausted, yet he felt happy at completing his project. He had gotten a good night's sleep and felt chipper the next morning at breakfast. Jane and Eddie stopped by the table where the interns were eating. Eddie smiled and said, "Good morning." Everyone noticed, as it was usually Jane who was the first to greet them.

They all nodded.

Eddie said, "When you're ready, please stop by my lab. No big deal. Whenever you're ready."

All the interns except Thebe grabbed their trays and jumped up. Marcos was about to walk his tray over to the clean-up area when he noticed that Thebe was still sitting and staring at his two remaining waffles. "Do you want to help save the world or have two more waffles?"

"I'm thinking," said Thebe. "These banana pecan waffles are especially good this morning."

"Come on, I give you permission to skip your manners, just this once," said Marcos.

Thebe put his knife and fork down, leaned over, and swallowed the two remaining waffles with one gulp.

"That's the spirit. Let's go."

Thebe grabbed his tray, put it in the clean-up area, and they headed out to catch up to the others.

All the interns entered Lab 51, Thebe being last closed the door. Eddie and Jane stood in front of a large dark gray tarp.

Eddie looked at the interns with a big grin. "You all know that a long time ago people didn't know what objects were made of. Then we figured out that everything is made up of atoms. A little while later we figured out that there is something even smaller than atoms, protons and neutrons. Then we figured out there are even smaller things, quarks and neutrinos. They are so small they can't be seen, even with our best microscopes. The next best thing is to see their tracks. Like waking up on a snowy morning to see deer tracks in the yard. You didn't see the deer, but you know they were there. Scientists have been tracking neutrinos for decades. They set up a specific area and wait to see if any neutrinos made a path. At first they observed the tracks in the ice at the South Pole. Then they decided to move the experiments to a more controllable location. They needed the correct material in order to see the tracks. Ideally the material would be plentiful, inexpensive, and thick enough for neutrinos to make collisions with the atoms in the material and the atoms that moved would show the path of the collisions. It would have to be a high density material so there would be lots of atoms to hit, but not solid or else you couldn't see through it. Water would be good but it's so clear you couldn't see the path. Scientists initially used tetrachloroethylene."

Everyone stared, including Jane.

"Sorry, that's plain old cleaning fluid used in dry cleaning as a spot remover. Surprise, surprise. Anyway, now they use liquid argon. It's more stable than cleaning fluid."

"So if atoms are too small to see…How small is a neutrino?" asked Liz.

"Sixty-five billion neutrinos pass through every square centimeter on Earth every second."

Everyone started looking at their bodies and looked a little worried.

"Not to worry," said Eddie. "If you walked through a valley you wouldn't hit the mountains would you? That's how small neutrinos and quarks are. Anyway, we don't want to just see the tracks, we want to capture the quarks."

"Why do we want to capture quarks?" asked Lu Lu.

"Because when things are that little, according to Einstein, they do 'spooky' things."

"I've got a little brother who does spooky things," said Marcos.

Everyone who had a little brother or sister nodded in agreement.

"Einstein used the term spooky?" asked Andy.

"Einstein said spooky," said Eddie. "In the normal world of big things, like trees and rocks, we have tested and re-tested their make-up and what they can do. Steel is steel and will always be steel. We can figure out how much we need to make a bridge. No surprises, it is always the same. However, at the quark level it does one thing that has baffled scientists for years..."

"Tell us," said John anxiously.

Everyone stared at Eddie.

"Quarks can be in two places at once."

There was silence in the room.

"No way," said Thebe.

"Oh yeah. Big way," said Eddie. "Part of our plan is to search for edible, fast growing, highly nutritious food on other planets. Jane has found a suitable exoplanet, but it is 5,000 light years away. Even if we developed a space ship that went at the speed of light, it would take 5,000 years to get there."

Marcos said, "So the round trip would take a really long time."

Everyone laughed.

Eddie continued, "Exactly. So we need a space ship that only takes a second. You all may have noticed the steady stream of Zoomerangs that have arrived here over the last few days. I called every neutrino tracking lab in the world and asked them to put thick layers of graphene at the end of their tracking stations. They all agreed and have collected and shipped quite a bit of what I call 'quark gel' to us. I have completed a small space ship and covered the outside with quark gel. Our space ship will be here…and then it will be there."

Everyone was excited.

Liz asked, "How do you steer it?"

"I set the galactic coordinates for the planet we want to visit in a GPS-like computer, hook the wires from the computer through the space ship and into the quark gel."

"And the quarks understand that?" asked Lu Lu.

"Apparently they do," responded Eddie. "Sort of like how sunlight hits a solar panel and the electrons know to flow along the skinny little wires in the panel to make electricity."

There was a stunned silence as everyone just stared.

Finally, John asked, "Does it work?"

"Oh yeah." Eddie pulled out the plastic container from the fridge and held up the pink mushrooms. "I took a little trip to Exoplanet 1 yesterday."

"Show us!" everyone begged.

"Hey, that's my line." Eddie put the mushrooms back in the fridge, took a couple of steps back, and pulled the tarp off his new machine.

The interns saw the glowing blue sphere and burst into applause.

Eddie looked as happy as new parents showing off their new-born baby.

"When do we go?" asked Marcos.

Eddie turned serious, "While we need to go to the exoplanet and explore for potential food, this exploration could be dangerous. The trip could be dangerous, the planet could be dangerous. That's why this exploration is a voluntary trip. Every important trip in the past has relied on volunteers, whether it was Christopher Columbus's crew or the first astronauts. I made the first test run and found the trip to be fine and the planet to be fine. However, you never know. That's why I want you to think about this and let me know if you prefer not to go, for any reason. There are plenty of other things that need to be done. So please, don't feel bad if you would prefer not to go on this trip. Take your time, think about it."

There was silence for one second.

Immediately, every hand went up. "We want to go," they all said.

CHAPTER 39

Eddie wanted to take all the interns on a quick 'test drive' just to make them familiar with the controls.

Before everyone got in the spaceship, Jane said, "Let's insert some safety rules. Only three interns at a time."

Everyone groaned.

Jane said, "Headquarters tells us that Eddie and I can't be on the same expedition together, just in case something goes wrong. Same thinking applies to the rule where the President of the U.S. and the Vice President can't travel together. Same thing here."

Everyone nodded.

Jane then asked Eddie, "How long will you be gone?"

"I don't know. Maybe a couple of minutes."

"How long were you gone last time?"

"Just a few seconds."

"What's the maximum amount of time that you think you could be gone?"

"I don't know."

Jane furrowed her brow as she looked straight at Eddie.

"You know, the Earth is spinning at 1670 kilometers per hour, but the Space Zoo 1 will be in the same place. How fast is Exo 1 spinning? How will the quarks know which path to take to come home?"

"I don't know. I think they just know."

"You're putting a lot of faith in physics."

"Well atoms have stuck together for 13 billion years and gravity has been working for 13 billion years. So, yeah, it seems like the universe has got it figured out. We're just taking a trip to the new grocery store."

"5,000 light years away."

"We're not disrupting the laws of nature."

"You kind of are."

Andy spoke up, "Is this one of those philosophical debates that could take hours?"

Jane and Eddie looked at each other.

Finally Eddie said, "We're going."

Eddie and the three closest interns, Marcos, Thebe, and Lu Lu, jumped into the spaceship. "I built this for seven, so we have plenty of room." He then closed the door.

Poof, they were gone.

Andy, John, Liz, and Jane were still in Lab 51.

"That's the first time I've seen you and Captain Eddie disagree. Don't scientists usually agree on everything?" asked Liz.

"Oh my, no," Jane said and shook her head. "Sometimes scientists disagree for decades. People do experiments, they write papers, and hold conferences, all the while disagreeing about some small point. Everybody has their say, and finally some sort of evidence usually presents itself that makes it obvious that one side of the debate is the right way to go. After years of discussion, they finally made Pluto a planet again. I mean for goodness sake, it has its own moons. People disagree about almost everything." She looked at the interns, "For example, what is the best topping for a pizza?"

"Oh that's easy," said, Andy, "it's plain with extra cheese."

"No way, it's sardines," said John.

"Not sardines again," said Liz.

"Try it," he said.

"See what I mean?" said Jane.

Poof, the spaceship was back.

The original three climbed out and the next three climbed in.

Poof, they were gone.

In a minute they were back and they all climbed out.

"Not bad, eh?" asked Eddie.

"At the risk of sounding like a spoiled kid," said Marcos, "again, again, again."

Eddie laughed, "We'll all go again soon."

"First," said Jane, "we'll have to come up with a checklist of exactly what to do on each trip. And a safety checklist."

"But first, the important stuff. What do we call our new spaceship?" asked Thebe.

"I call it the Quark Based Overthruster," said Eddie. Everyone stared. Eddie knew he wasn't expecting applause, but he didn't expect silence.

"That's a mouthful," said Jane.

"How about Intergalactic Business Machine?" asked John.

"I think the legal department would say no," said Jane.

"How about The Spooky Machine?" asked Andy.

"That sounds too...spooky," said Liz. "How about The Quark Master 3000?"

"Someone's been staying up too late and watching too many infomercials," said Lu Lu.

"How about Quark Thruster?" suggested John.

"Better," said Jane.

Marcos went over to the whiteboard and picked up a marker. He wrote, Quark Based Overthruster, then underlined a few letters, <u>Quark</u> Based Overthrust<u>er</u>.

"Quarker." he said.

"I like it," said Eddie.

"Me too," said Jane.

"Yeah," said Andy.

Everyone else applauded.

"Quarker it is," smiled Eddie.

CHAPTER 40

After lunch, everyone met in the conference room.

"All right," Eddie started. "Jane and I have come up with a checklist for everyone who goes to the exoplanet or Exo 1. We are calling it Exo 1 because we assume we will travel to an Exo 2 and Exo 3 in the near future."

Everyone grinned and nodded.

Jane clicked the remote so that each item would appear on the screen as Eddie explained them.

"Number one – grab a sample of a fruit or vegetable, put it in your backpack.

Number two – take a picture of the area.

Number three – don't stay longer than five minutes.

Number four – take your sample to the bio lab.

Number five – post your picture on the wall next to the Quarker under the time of the trip.

Number six – write up a report describing everything you saw, plants, animals, weather, etc.

And number seven – don't stay longer than five minutes."

"We thought of another one when we were at lunch," said John.

"Good," said Jane. "Let's hear it."

"Always wear your seatbelt. Eddie made us put them on when we went, but we should always remember that."

"Good point. Safety first," said Eddie.

"What happens in the bio lab?" asked Liz.

Jane responded, "We will analyze the new fruits or vegetables you bring back. The old method used centuries ago of analyzing newly discovered food to see if you could eat it was slightly helpful, but it didn't work every time. First they would look at the food to see that it didn't have any fungus, and that it wasn't a mushroom. Secondly they would smell it. The food shouldn't smell like almonds which indicates it might contain poison. Thirdly they would rub a small piece of the food on the inside of their wrist to see if any red bumps occurred. If bumps occurred, that might indicate that it would cause an allergic reaction in the stomach. After the microscope was invented, they would look at food under the microscope to see if it had bugs or worms living in the food. Now we place the food into the food analyzer and it tests for good things like proteins, carbohydrates, and fats, and bad things like poisons. If it's OK to eat, we'll try it in the cafeteria. If everyone likes it, we'll see if we can grow it in the hydroponic garden. If that works, we'll send it down to Earth."

"One of the botanists in the rainforest room used the expression 'non-native species.' Does that apply to the exoplanet food?" asked Lu Lu.

Eddie said, "The word native means it belongs there or it was there first. Whatever you find on the exoplanet, it is native to the exoplanet. When you bring it back to the Earth, it is non-native here. Non-native doesn't mean it is good or bad, it just means it's not from here. When we bring something back, we have to make sure we test it very thoroughly. One, as food, as Jane just described, and two, so we don't introduce things that could end up being harmful to our environment."

"How could a non-native species be harmful?" asked Liz.

Jane responded, "For an animal example, pythons were accidentally released into the Florida Everglades. They are very aggressive and are eating endangered birds. A plant example is Kudzu, which was introduced to North America in 1876 as a fast growing plant that would help reduce soil erosion. However, it grew so quickly that it has overrun and killed off many good native plants.

"So we must be careful to test everything we bring back," summarized Eddie.

"Are there ever good non-native species?" asked Thebe.

"Yes," responded Jane. "There have been several items that were originally non-native that have had great benefits. For example, honeybees, introduced to North America in 1622, and oats, and wheat, introduced in North America several hundred years ago, have proven to be very beneficial."

"Why should each trip only last five minutes?" asked Liz.

"We don't know," answered Jane, staring at Eddie.

"How can we find out?" asked Andy.

"I was just going to go and each time stay a little longer," ventured Eddie.

"And what if on the last trip you stay one minute too long?" asked Marcos.

"You guys ask a lot of questions. When I was interning I would have jumped at this opportunity."

Marcos said, "I think in one of your lectures you may have said something like, 'Ask a hundred questions and then ask a hundred more.' "

"Well, you caught me there. I'm proud of that quote."

"What if we come up with a way to figure out the answer?" asked Marcos.

"Good, I like that."

The other interns looked at Marcos, all of them with raised eyebrows.

John said, "These seem like important trips. Shouldn't we just go?"

Lu Lu jumped into the conversation and said, "I'm with Marcos. I don't like the idea of not coming back."

"OK. Here's my plan," said Marcos. "We build a robot, program it to push the return button in one minute. It returns and we reset it for two minutes and send it out again. It returns and we reset it for three minutes and send it out again. And so on."

"And eventually, on what will be its last trip it just might not return. What then?" asked John.

"Then we know the time limit of the trips, and we tell Eddie to build another one."

"Yeah, you tell him," said John.

Eddie had been off to the side with Jane, but was also listening to the interns' discussion, said, "That's actually a good idea. Some of you should build a robot, and some of you should test the pink mushrooms in the lab to see if they grow here. I already tested them in the bio lab. They're safe. I'll build another Quarker."

The interns got up and headed to the labs.

CHAPTER 41

Marcos, Thebe, and Lu Lu went off to Lab 2 to work on the robot. Liz, Andy, and John headed over to the bio lab to work on the pink mushrooms.

Marcos said, "Let's pick up a cart in Lab 2, then we can go to the other labs to look for parts that might help us."

They spent the next few hours rummaging through all the other labs, picking up parts, discussing them, then either putting them back or placing them on the cart. They got back to Lab 2 and Thebe said, "I'm hungry for lunch but I'd rather stay here and put this guy together."

"Me too," said Lu Lu.

"I agree," said Marcos. "Pity we don't have room service up here."

Thebe said, "Once we make the robot, we can send it out for lunch."

Marcos and Lu Lu laughed.

They immediately started assembling the parts. After another couple of hours, it was finished. They stood back and admired their work. It looked small, raggedy, and none of the parts matched.

"Perfect," said Marcos.

"How do we test it?" asked Thebe.

"Let's see if the voice recognition system works," suggested Lu Lu.

Marcos and Thebe nodded.

"Hello. Hello. Robot can you hear us?" said Lu Lu.

No response.

Marcos looked at it for a moment, then reached over and pushed the 'on' button. "When I was a kid, my parents paid for the TV repairperson to come 'fix' the TV, when all he needed to do was plug it back in."

"Been there," said Thebe.

Lu Lu tried again, "Hello. Hello. Robot can you hear us?"

"Yes, I hear you," the robot said.

Marcos, Thebe, and Lu Lu were all smiles.

The accent was that of a Russian female.

"Do you know where the cafeteria is?" asked Thebe.

Lu Lu elbowed Thebe and mouthed "Stop it." Then laughed.

Lu Lu turned to Marcos and Thebe, "Where did the voice recognition system come from?"

Thebe said, "I found that part. I think I remember the stamp on the back said Russia. Probably left over from one of their earlier space projects. I remember reading Walstib bought every spare part from every space project from every country."

"Who assembled your voice recognition system?" asked Marcos.

All the parts electronically interconnected with the robot's computer unit when the interns put it together.

"Searching," said the robot. After a few seconds, it said, "My records show the VRS unit was assembled by Yelena."

"Yelena, that's a nice name. Mind if we call you Yelie?" asked Lu Lu.

"That is acceptable," said the robot.

"Yelie. Do you like to travel?" asked Thebe.

CHAPTER 42

Liz, Andy, and John walked into the bio lab. Carlos, a guinea pig name after Carlos Noriega, an astronaut from Peru, was working on an experiment.

"Hi Carlos. Can we set up an experiment?" asked Liz.

"Sure, give me a second. I was just about to steam clean some of Pete's dishes."

"Don't you mean Petri dish?" asked John.

"Just kidding you," he smiled. He finished loading the Petri dishes into the steam cleaner and closed the door. "There, they will be clean in a few moments. What are you all testing?"

"To see if we can get the mushroom seeds from the exoplanet to grow," said Andy.

"You mean mushroom spores. Mushrooms grow from spores," corrected Carlos.

Andy held up the mushrooms and popped out a seed the size of a walnut, "That's not a spore, that's a seed."

Carlos held his paw out, "May I?"

"Of course," said Andy and handed over the seed.

Carlos took the seed, climbed up onto the lab table, placed it under a large microscope, and looked into the eyepiece. "Ahhh. We are both right. Take a look." He flicked a switch and what he saw under the microscope was now showing on the video monitor.

Liz, Andy, and John looked in amazement as Carlos explained. "There appears to be thousands of spores tightly packed into one large seed."

"Why not just spores?" asked Liz.

"Don't know," replied Carlos. "Why are you conducting the experiment here and not in the hydroponics garden?"

"We have to conduct this experiment away from all the other plants in the hydroponics garden just in case this plant has any bad germs that would contaminate the other plants that are already growing and healthy," said Andy.

"Why? Where are they from?" asked Carlos.

"The exoplanet we're researching," said Liz.

"Sure, sure," scoffed Carlos. "You interns are always joking. So are you going to use a grow-stay?"

"What's that?" asked John. "We thought we'd put the seeds in three different types of soil in a planter and keep an eye on which one worked best."

"A grow-stay is a growing station. It is all stainless steel equipment that is surrounded by plastic drapes. It starts out super clean so nothing here contaminates your seeds. There are several over there." He pointed across the lab. "Bet you never thought to worry that we might contaminate your new plants."

"We never thought of that. But thank you very much for your advice," said Liz. "We'll make sure we don't get any of Pete's dishes messy from our experiment."

Carlos smiled. "That sounds like a great experiment. Hope it goes well. See you in the morning. Call me if you need any help," said Carlos as he left the lab.

The interns set up a growing-station and placed plastic drapes around the grow-stay. It looked like a hospital room.

"We have three seeds," said Liz. "Let's try two in soil in pots and one in a hydroponic trough."

"But we don't have all the tubing," said John.

"Remember how you would grow an avocado in class in school? We just stick some toothpicks in the mushroom seed and put it on top of a glass jar filled with water and see if the roots are drawn to the water. It doesn't have to be set up to make the seed grow for weeks or months, just long enough to see if the roots grow."

"Sounds good," said Andy.

It took just a short while to set everything up.

"OK, everything looks in place," said Andy.

The interns then set up a makeshift viewing area in the bio-lab. There was a folding chair with a cup holder, just like the ones used while watching sporting events. They also found a couple of cots, a cooler, and a lamp. Obviously others had stayed overnight to keep watch over their experiments.

"If we're going to be here all night watching the seeds, it looks like we'll miss dinner," said Andy. "I'll go get some snacks and drinks."

"Thanks," said John and Liz.

Andy returned quickly and put some drinks in the cooler.

"I've got limeade, a sandwich, and I found a neat biology notebook. I'm all set to take the first watch," said John.

"Wake me in a couple of hours for my turn," said Andy.

"I'll take the shift after that," said Liz.

"It's good that we're here. If something goes wrong, we will be right here to help," said John.

"I hope nothing goes wrong. We only have three seeds to test," said Liz.

"Nothing will go wrong," said Andy.

"We've set up a good experiment. We've got three separate grow-stays. We've labeled them properly, 'hard soil,' 'loose soil,' and 'hydroponic.' And, we made the pots out of glass boxes, so we should be able to see any root growth."

They all stared at the three seeds.

"What kind of time frame should we expect?" asked John.

"Tomatoes, avocados, and corn each take about ten days before seeds sprout roots," said Liz. "However, Eddie did say there looked to be billions of these. So they must grow fairly quickly. Some fungi on earth can grow overnight." They continued to stare.

"Get to bed. I'll be here," said John.

They all said good night.

"I wish they'd all grow," said Liz, as she lay on her cot.

"Wishing won't help," said Andy.

"Wishing couldn't hurt."

"So says the one who likes romantic movies," said Andy.

"You like them too," she said, and gave a little smile.

John took another look at the grow-stays, smiled, sat in the folding chair, and opened the notebook. He read a few pages and looked up. Nothing had changed. He read another few pages and looked up again. No root growth. He stood up and looked at the gauges. Each grow-stay had gauges for moisture and light levels. All levels were in the 'normal' range.

He sat back down and continued reading. He read another few pages and looked up. Again, no root growth. He read another few pages, then stared at the seeds again. Nothing. "Oh well," he sighed, and started to read again.

A few minutes later he looked up at the bottom half of the grow-stays and saw a massive tangle of roots. He took a deep breath and looked up at the top half. What he saw shocked him.

The mushrooms had grown so tall they were growing out of the grow-stays and were looking directly at him. Then they leaned over closer to him and called his name. "John, John, John."

John responded, "What do you need? Are you thirsty? Do you need more water? Are you hungry? Do you need more plant food?"

The mushrooms continued to chant at him, "John, John, John."

John jolted awake.

Andy stood over him, "John, wake up."

"Yes, yes I'm awake," John said as he rubbed his eyes.

"Hey buddy, you fell asleep. Who were you talking to?"

John looked at the grow-stays. Still no root growth.

"Unfortunately, nobody."

"It's my turn to keep watch. You can grab some time on the cot."

John closed the notebook, stood up, went over to the cot, and went back to sleep.

The next morning, John and Andy woke up and joined Liz. They stood together and stared at the seeds. Nothing.

"This could be a long experiment," said Liz.

Just then they heard what sounded like the faintest pop one could ever hear. Then a little pink root ventured out of the seed in the hydroponic grow-stay. Then another pop, and the seed in the loose soil sprouted. Then a second later, another pop and the seed in the hard-packed soil sprouted. John, Liz, and Andy let out loud cheers. Then they looked at the clock and realized it was still early, well before breakfast. They did silent high-fives.

CHAPTER 43

All the interns dragged themselves to the cafeteria having gotten little or no sleep.

"Now I see why they make the 'time to go to sleep' announcement every night," said Thebe.

They all nodded, slowly, in agreement, and didn't say another word the rest of breakfast.

Eddie and Jane came by their table.

"Good morning," said Jane, sounding way too chipper.

"Any results?" asked Eddie.

They all nodded, slowly.

"Good. When you've finished breakfast, let's all go to Lab 2 first, then to the bio lab. We'll have a good old-fashioned show and tell."

After they finished breakfast, Eddie, Jane, and all the Interns gathered at Lab 2.

Marcos, Thebe, and Lu Lu walked over to Yelie. Lu Lu pushed the on button.

"Hello, Yelie," said Marcos.

"Hello, Marcos," said Yelie.

"Been any place special lately?" asked Thebe.

"I have been to Exo 1 thirty-seven times," said Yelie.

"And what did we conclude?" asked Marcos.

"There is no time limit. You do not have to worry about the rotation of the exoplanet. On the way there, the Quarker lands on the outermost portion of the planet. On the way back, the Quarker goes through the planet. In a straight line between here and there, it also goes through about a hundred other planets."

"I understand how a single quark, being so small, goes through everything else," said Jane. "How do we, the passengers, go through everything?"

Eddie took a deep breath, "When you go as fast as the speed of light, you cease to have any mass, or weight, or size. You are pure energy. You can go through anything. Quarks travel instantaneously, which is perhaps a million times the speed of light. Hard to imagine. So let's just say that for one billionth of a second you cease to exist in your present form and you can go through anything."

"Yes, hard to imagine," said Jane slowly.

"When you sneeze, your body changes your heart beat to compensate for the pressure in the body from the sneeze. It is very brief, the heart doesn't stop, and obviously you don't die. When we travel instantaneously, we are pure energy for less than a billionth of a second. Probably not even enough time for the heart to change a beat, and obviously we don't die." Eddie smiled.

"Now you tell me," said Yelie.

Everyone laughed.

"She's developed a bit of a sense of humor," said Marcos.

"Excellent experiment," said Jane. "Let's head to the bio lab."

Andy, Liz, and John described how their experiment was set up. The roots had actually grown a little more while they had been at breakfast.

"This too is an excellent experiment," said Eddie. "These roots have grown really fast. No wonder there were so many mushrooms. Once we get them to Earth, we'll have to make sure to keep them from spreading where they shouldn't."

"I have a thought," said Andy. "Experimenting with different soils seems to take a lot of time and a lot of effort. I think a new requirement on the checklist should be to gather a soil sample when we gather a vegetable or fruit sample. We could analyze the soil when we get back and it would tell us how to duplicate the soil instead of having to do an experiment each time."

"Eddie, you won't get mad if we add to your checklist," asked Liz.

"I would think he'd be furious," said Jane.

All the interns looked a little nervous.

Eddie slapped his tail, and said, "I'm furious."

Jane looked at the interns and mouthed "Told you so."

"That's brilliant. Yes, add it to the checklist. I'm furious with myself for not thinking of that."

Jane went over to Eddie and said, "There, there. You poor dear. You thought of a way to travel thousands of light years away but forgot to add taking a trowel and a plastic bag for soil to the checklist. Yes, I'd be furious with myself too. Let's go to the Captain's Lounge and get you a big scoop of your favorite chunky mango sorbet." Jane smiled at the interns, "These were brilliant experiments. You all are invited to the Lounge too."

A few minutes later, in the Captain's Lounge, Jane went to get everyone a scoop of sorbet. Eddie leaned over to the interns, "Works every time. I pretend to get mad, and she lets me go off my diet."

Jane returned with a tray of bowls filled with chunky mango sorbet, and passed them out.

"Cheers to you all for your experiments. Bon appetite," said Eddie as he winked and took a big bite of the sorbet.

CHAPTER 44

After a snack of chunky mango sorbet, Liz and Andy decided to go on a 'quick trip' to Exo 1. 'Quick trip' was the new term, as they had all agreed that thirty minutes would be the maximum time for now. The Quarker was still new. The trips were still new. And Exo 1 still had not been fully explored. Each trip was still potentially dangerous. But, everyone agreed, the benefits of helping the people of Earth, still outweighed the potential danger. Liz and Andy landed on Exo 1, and got out of their Quarker.

They saw fields that stretched out for about several kilometers of waist-high something. It looked like tall grass, waving in the breeze.

They walked through it.

"I thought this was like wheat because it's yellow, but it's more like tall, thin asparagus," said Liz.

Andy reached over and snapped off the tip of one of the stalks.

"Look, it's got juice coming out of it." He sniffed it. "It smells like lemon and banana."

"I'll take a picture of the field," said Liz. She pulled out her camera and took several long-range pictures and a few close-ups of the stalk.

"Do you have any metal wire?" she asked.

"What for?"

"I want to try an experiment."

Andy looked in his pockets, he found a spiral paper notebook and a pen. "How about the spiral part of my notebook?"

"Yes. Great. Can you pull it off the notebook?"

"OK, but I still don't…"

"I'll show you in a second," Liz interrupted. "Just pull the wire off and bend it till it breaks into two halves."

Andy bent the wire back and forth till it broke in two and handed both pieces to her.

Liz opened the back of the camera. She talked as she performed her experiment.

"I noticed my camera battery was a little low. So, remember those experiments we did in school where you light up a light bulb by putting wires into a potato or a lemon?"

"Yes. Those were fun."

Liz stuck the two wires into a stalk and then held the other ends onto the battery in the camera.

"How long will this take?" asked Andy.

"I don't know. Let's give it a minute. That mango sorbet was delicious. What's your favorite food?"

"Probably bark and grass cream pie," smiled Andy. "What's yours?"

"I guess eucalyptus smoothies."

Liz looked at her camera. "The camera showed a fifty-four percent charge before. Now the gauge shows fifty-five percent. Now fifty-six."

"We don't have to wait till it's fully charged do we?"

"No. I was just checking. They say that physics is physics, no matter where you are in the universe. Now we know that's true. Whether it's the Earth, the Moon, or an exoplanet." Liz put away her camera and handed back the two wires to Andy.

He put the wires back in his pocket with all the loose paper. All of a sudden a long, pink stretchy object shot past them and landed on the broken-off stalk. Just as quickly, it snapped back.

They looked at the stalk. There were hundreds of small bugs, about the size of Lady Bugs, that had gathered to eat the juice from the stalk. But there was a section where there were no bugs, and in their place was a thick film of green slime. They then looked over to where the pink thing came from and saw a huge frog about the size of an elephant standing about five meters away. There was green slime dripping from its mouth.

"He was really quiet," noted Liz quietly. She tried not to move.

"Yeah. We were talking though. Look at how big his nostrils are. He must have smelled the juice from some distance away, and known that there would be a meal of bugs."

"He's got a huge smile. He's kind of cute."

The huge, long, pink tongue shot out of the frog's mouth and landed on Liz. Andy grabbed her arm with his hand. The tongue tried to recoil but Andy held firm. The tongue gave another tug and it pulled Liz half a meter.

"Cute and strong," said Andy, as he stared at the tongue stuck on Liz.

"Please do something," said Liz in a very serious tone.

"I'm thinking."

"Reach into your pocket, get the pieces of wire, and jab its tongue," she said in an urgent tone.

"I don't want to hurt it."

"I'm about to join the bugs for his lunch," said Liz in a very urgent tone.

Still holding onto Liz with one arm, Andy reached into his other pocket with his other hand, and pulled out a sandwich. He pried off the top slice of bread with his thumb, let it drop, and mushed the remainder of the sandwich onto the frog's tongue.

The tongue let go and the frog hopped away.

"Whew…thanks," said Liz. "What was in your sandwich?"

"Ciabatta bread, tomatoes from the hydroponic garden, and a healthy slathering of spicy mustard."

"I'm glad you like spicy food."

"I'm glad that guy doesn't."

"Why did you have a sandwich?"

"I made it at breakfast. I was still so tired from last night, I made the sandwich before I realized we were at breakfast. I jammed in into my pocket and had the pancakes which looked far more breakfast-y."

"Are you awake now?"

'Very much awake."

"Let's gather some stalks and some soil, and get out of here," said Liz.

Liz snapped off a few stalks, and Andy filled a sample bag with some soil. They jumped into the Quarker and headed back.

CHAPTER 45

The interns sat in the cafeteria eating dinner.

John said, "I know Jane has asked us how we got our interest in science. But I missed a few of those conversations when I was doing my spacewalk introduction. Thebe, would you mind telling your story again?"

"Not at all. I had a lot of other interesting classes, but I think it was just that my biology teacher had such a love for biology, it made everyone in the class really like it," responded Thebe. He continued, "I think there are things about science that most scientists like. For example the idea that if you work hard enough you can get the exact answer."

"Like two plus two equals four," suggested Marcos.

"Yes," continued Thebe. "It's a good feeling to get the right answer."

"I agree," said Lu Lu.

"Scientists have been working on string theory and particle physics and other areas for years, and no one has an answer yet. How about those scientists who like working on things for which, right now, there are no right answers? asked John.

"I guess, for many, the search is the thing," said Thebe.

"The early explorers had no idea what they were looking for. They just loved the search," said Lu Lu.

"Some people complain that everything has already been found," sighed John.

"I think we are just scratching the surface," said Andy.

"I just found the last slice of pizza. Anyone else want it?" asked Thebe.

CHAPTER 46

After Liz and Andy returned from their trip, Jane gathered all the interns in the conference room. "Now that we have a little exoplanet experience under our belts, I'd like to add another item to the checklist. Eddie's not here, he doesn't need any more desserts."

The interns laughed.

"As a navigator, I like knowing where things are. Currently when you go to Exo 1, you take a picture. That gives a good picture of what to expect when the next person climbs out of the Quarker. I'd like to add to that by mapping the planet."

"That sounds like fun," said John.

"I hope so," said Jane. "There is a long history of scientists and explorers seeking new things and creating maps so others might follow. Christopher Columbus left from Spain in 1492 and looked for trade routes to China, but without a map, he bumped into North America. Prince Henry of Portugal created maps of Western Africa in the 1400s mostly looking for gold. Ferdinand Magellan of Spain was the first to plan a circumnavigation of the world in the early 1500s. Sir Francis Drake of England was the first to complete it start to finish in 1577, using Magellan's maps. The Lewis and Clark expedition in 1804 created detailed maps of the western portion of the United States. People began mapping the Moon with telescopes in1645 and used satellites with cameras to film the far side of the Moon in 1959. People were mapping Mars with telescopes in the 1600s and spacecraft went there in the 1960s. We'll continue that tradition by sending up drones with wide angle cameras for photographing the geography of the planet, and GPRs for inspecting the geology of the planet."

"What's a GPR?" asked Lu Lu.

"Ground penetrating radars. As we know from studying bats, radar sends a pulse out, it hits something, and the pulse is sent back. The bat can tell from the way the pulse comes back whether it's a mosquito in the air or a tree. The GPR pulses go down and bounce back and the results then show up on the computer screen. If you see a steady line then it's plain soil, and if there's a wavy line then it shows there are diffractors, meaning something else that deflects the radar pulses differently, like a rock, or a dinosaur bone, different geological formations, or water, or a cave."

"How far down do the pulses go?" asked Liz.

"The GPR, when first introduced, could only send pulses down fifteen meters but ours can go down about two hundred meters. If the drones find something that we like, we can go back to the same place and explore it in person."

"Very cool," said Thebe.

"Consider it on the list," said John.

"I hope we have enough drones," laughed Marcos.

CHAPTER 47

A few days later, Thebe and Marcos returned from a mapping trip to the exoplanet. They jumped out of their Quarker and immediately texted all the other interns, "Get to the Quarker as fast as you can."

In a few moments all the other interns arrived at Lab 51. Marcos and Thebe said "Jump in. You have to see this."

Lu Lu said, "But they said we all couldn't go together."

"I know" said Marcos, "But this is amazing. We'll be back in one minute."

They all climbed aboard. Thebe was the last to get in and it was a tight squeeze, his butt was sticking out and the door wouldn't close. "I'm on the treadmill daily. I'm working on it," exclaimed Thebe. They gave him a tug and the door closed. They pushed the green button and headed out.

When they arrived at the exoplanet, they flung open the door and hopped out. They gazed at the most magnificent view they had ever seen. It extended for several kilometers. They were up on a slight hill and the landscape below was filled with mushrooms of every color, some were over fifty meters tall. Dragonflies with ten-meter wingspans flew in and out of the mushrooms trying to catch very flimsy looking jellyfish that were floating with the breeze, like a school of fish.

John spoke up, "Remember when I said some people feel that everything has already been discovered?"

Everyone nodded but kept staring out at the view.

"Well, they are really wrong."

They kept staring.

"How do you bring back a fifty meter mushroom?" asked Andy.

"We're gonna need a bigger Quarker," said Marcos.

Two dragonflies pulled at the same jellyfish. A breeze swept through the mushrooms and they swayed.

"We should get back," said Lu Lu.

"One more minute," implored Thebe.

They kept staring at the beautiful scene.

After a minute, they reluctantly climbed back in.

When they arrived back in Lab 51, Eddie and Jane were waiting.

Jane tapped her talons on the floor and stared directly at them. Eddie thumped his tail.

Jane spoke up, "Rules are there for your safety, not to be mean."

"It was my fault," said Marcos. "I talked them into the trip."

"What was so important that you thought breaking the rules was worth it?" asked Jane.

Lu Lu held out her camera. Jane took a look. "Wow. I need to go on some trips." She showed the camera to Eddie.

"Wow is right. Best trip with a view ever. You go on the next trip."

Eddie looked at the interns, "Yes, that was spectacular. You are grounded. Instead of any trips today and tomorrow, you stay here in my lab and help me finish Quarker 2." He pointed to a second tarp in another part of the lab.

They all hung their heads down to hide their smiles.

"That doesn't seem like punishment to them," said Jane.

"OK, said Eddie, "No sorbet for a day as well."

"Doesn't the Constitution forbid cruel and unusual punishment?" asked Thebe.

CHAPTER 48

All the interns could talk about at dinner was the amazing view they had seen earlier or the size of the new Quarker 2. They had asked for a bigger version, and they were getting it. Everyone was chatting but Lu Lu. She nodded occasionally to keep the others from interrupting her concentration. She was lost in thought.

After dinner, Andy said, "Who wants to hit the gym?" Everyone agreed, but Lu Lu said, "You all go ahead. I'll meet up with you later."

Lu Lu walked slowly to the bridge. She went up to Eddie and Jane and said, "I have a question."

They noticed a softness to the statement, not the usual peppy tone.

Eddie and Jane leaned back in their seats to give her their full attention. "Anything in particular?" asked Jane.

"It's not a science question," she responded.

"Ahhh," said Jane. She knew that occasionally, interns had questions about the big picture. Seeing all the new technology. Seeing the beauty of the Earth. Seeing the scale of the projects they worked on. Eventually, it got almost every member of the Space Zoo team to thinking about where they fit in. Jane looked at Eddie, "Should I take her to see Charlize?"

"I thinks that's a good idea," said Eddie very calmly.

"Follow me," said Jane. She took Lu Lu to the right side of the bridge and opened one of the small panel doors.

"I thought this was for electrical wiring and air ducts," said Lu Lu.

"Most of these are," said Jane. Once they were inside the wall, there were several smaller doors labeled, 'electrical,' 'water pipes,' etc. There was one door that had no label.

Jane opened that one. They walked down a surprisingly wide hall that seemed to angle upwards, until it came to another door. Jane knocked.

They heard a pleasant voice say, "Come in."

Jane opened the door and they walked in. The room was filled with antiques from all over the world, including an antique globe, antique maps on the wall, old leather books, and a model of an old sailing ship named Beagle.

And, sitting at an antique wooden desk in front of a round porthole looking out at the Earth, was a huge, very old tortoise.

Jane looked at the female tortoise, named after Charles Darwin, and said, "Charlize, this is Lu Lu, one of our interns." Jane looked at Lu Lu, "Lu Lu, this is Charlize, one of the original members of the Space Zoo Patrol team. She's traveled to every country on Earth, and knows a thing or two."

Lu Lu nodded respectfully.

"Greetings," said Charlize.

"I have to get back to the bridge. See you later," said Jane as she left the room.

'Where are you from?" asked Charlize.

"I'm from Shandong Province in China. How about you?"

"I'm from the Galapagos Islands." She pointed out the window, "Just a little water separates where we came from."

Lu Lu felt a closeness to Charlize. She felt she could ask her anything. "I have a question," she stated.

"Ask away," Charlize said, lightheartedly.

"All of us interns just went to the exoplanet that Jane found. We saw the most amazing sight I will ever see. It got me to thinking. Where did it all come from?"

"Probably the Big Bang."

"Why did you say probably?"

"Well 99.999 per cent of all our theories, observations, and experiments point to the Big Bang as the start. But, as you know, we weren't there. So, we didn't have a direct observation."

Lu Lu realized that she was being funny and gave a smile back.

"But what started the Big Bang?"

"I have two theories."

"What are they?" Lu Lu shot in eagerly.

"The first is that in the last universe, all the old stars and planets collapsed into black holes each with massive gravitational pulls. And eventually, all the black holes, billions and billions of them, pulled each other into one giant black hole, which then collapsed, becoming the Big Crunch. And then, one billionth of a second later after it couldn't collapse anymore, the Big Bang happened and started this universe."

"So this is universe number two?"

"Or, it could be universe number 2000. This could have been going on for trillions of years."

"On and on like a slinky?"

"Yes, we'll call it the slinky universe theory," Charlize said and smiled at Lu Lu.

Lu Lu stared out the window into space for a minute. "Hard to imagine and yet hard not to imagine."

"A lot of scientists think about this all the time," added Charlize.

"What is your second theory?" asked Lu Lu.

"God clapped his hands."

"So you believe in God?"

"I think a lot of scientists do."

"Do religious people believe in science?"

"I think most do."

"Well what's the difference between science and religion?" asked Lu Lu.

"The way I think about it, is that science is the study of things and how to try to make them work better. And religion provides a framework to help people get along better."

"A lot of people seem to think that science is difficult, but when you put it like that, science sounds easier than trying to understand people."

"People don't seem to get along sometimes. They could probably learn a thing or two from us animals. Maybe that's why Walstib only selected animals to be up here." Charlize paused for a moment, "You posed an interesting question, I'm glad you came up here."

"Thank you for some interesting answers."

"You're welcome. And I hope we will talk again soon."

"I hope I didn't interrupt you."

"No, no. I was just doing a little reading."

"I like reading, too"

"Come back again soon and we can swap stories about what we've read."

Lu Lu said, "See you soon then," and headed out the door.

CHAPTER 49

The next day, the interns spent their last day of being grounded helping Eddie complete Quarker 2.

At the end of the day, the interns sat in the cafeteria eating their dinner.

Thebe said, "Great day in the lab, today."

Lu Lu nodded and said, "I agree."

They continued to eat and relax.

After a few minutes, Lu Lu continued, "Thebe if you could go anywhere and do anything for one hour, what would it be?"

"I don't know. I'd have to think about it."

"That's easy," said Dave. "I would go to Laika's Lovey Dovey Doggy Day Spa for a one-hour belly rub."

"That sounds fun," said Lu Lu.

Thebe said, "OK. I got this. I would get a mud bath. Everything up here is too sterile."

Marcos asked, "Does it have to be back on earth?"

"No, it can be anywhere," responded Lu Lu.

"Then I would go jetpacking through the canyons of Mars," Marcos said, while he swerved his body as if he was already jetpacking.

"I heard that's pretty cool," added Andy. "How about you Lu Lu?"

"I'd go back to my parent's house and have a huge bowl of their bamboo stew."

"Is bamboo all you eat?" asked Liz.

"Mostly, but sometimes I have sugar cane or apples."

"I'm done with dinner. Let's continue this discussion at the gym," said John.

Everyone nodded then took their trays up to the clean-up area. As they headed to the gym, Thebe suggested, "Let's sign a petition to get a day spa up here."

CHAPTER 50

The next day was a lecture day and after breakfast everyone went to the conference room.

Once everyone was seated, Eddie started, "Today we'll discuss the different layers that make up the crust of the Earth."

Marcos raised his hand.

Eddie pointed at Marcos, "Yes."

"I don't mean to interrupt, but in our first lecture, you discussed the 'scientific method.' What is the other method?"

"What do you mean?"

"Well, if there is a scientific method, there must be another method that isn't the scientific method."

Eddie thought for a moment, "That's a good question. The scientific method refers to a very methodical way to approach the discovery process, or more generally, the learning process. I suppose one could call the other method the 'regular learning method' or the 'usual method' or the 'every-day method,' although I don't think anyone has ever used those expressions. On a daily basis we receive knowledge that simply gets stored in our brain's memory banks and then we use the information as needed."

"In the scientific method, we do experiments. Where does this knowledge come from for the other method?" asked Liz.

"It comes from everywhere, like the news, books, movies, folklore, mythology, local customs, beliefs, rituals, stories. Even going for a walk, you absorb what is going on. Is every story one hundred percent accurate? Probably not. They don't have to be. They can still teach us valuable lessons."

"Such as?" asked Andy.

"How about an old fable, such as 'Jack and the Beanstalk.' That was one of my favorites growing up. Is that a true story?"

Everyone shook their heads or said, "No."

"But you still learned a lesson, stealing is bad."

"But Jack wasn't stealing, he was just getting the things back that the giant stole from the village," said Lu Lu.

Eddie smiled, "If the giant stole those things, then stealing is bad?"

"Yes," said John.

"The way the story was originally written, the giant owned those things and Jack saw an opportunity to help his parents and the village by stealing from the giant. So, if Jack stole those things, is stealing bad?"

"Still yes," said John.

"Exactly," said Eddie. "A valuable lesson and a fun story either way."

"Thank you," said Marcos, 'but we still don't have a name for the usual-every-day-unscientific-method."

"Let's make that a homework assignment. For now, let's discuss the Earth's crust."

"Can you tell it as a fun story?" asked Marcos.

"Sure," said Eddie. "The Earth's crust occasionally needs to eject foreign matter, like molten rock, or magma, so the Earth forms a volcano to pop it out. Just like on our skin when we need to eject foreign matter, like bacteria, the skin forms a pimple to pop it out."

"EEEEEWWWWW!" said everyone.

"Just tell us about the crust. It's OK to skip the story," said Marcos.

Eddie proceeded to discuss the igneous rocks, sedimentary rocks, and metamorphic rocks that make up the Earth's crust. Everyone listened carefully the rest of the day.

CHAPTER 51

Marcos and Thebe teamed up for another trip to Exo 1.
They set the coordinates, they pushed the button, and off
they went. They landed on the exoplanet and immediately
climbed out. They looked around and saw a stream of
water.

"Let's follow the water to see where it leads," said Marcos.
After a few steps, Thebe lost his footing and lurched
forward. Luckily he caught his balance.

Marcos jumped over to Thebe to help steady him and
asked, "Are you all right? What happened?"

Thebe looked back and said, "I'm fine, thanks. I tripped
over that root, but I didn't see it before I walked there."
They saw the root shimmy itself back under the surface.
They stared in disbelief, then took another cautious step
forward. Sure enough, as their feet put pressure on the
ground, the root shimmied just enough to break the surface.

"That's weird," said Thebe.

They took another cautious step and the next part of the
root also came up.

"Let's follow the root," said Marcos.

The root veered away from the stream and they continued
to follow it one steady step at a time. After about a quarter
of a kilometer, they came across hundreds of large plants
that looked like Venus flytraps, except they all lay on the
ground. When Marcos and Thebe walked closer to the
plants, their footsteps put pressure on the ground and the
plants, like the roots, rose up. The plants rose to about two
meters tall. The part that looked like a Venus flytrap
opened up, and inside there were large round objects that
looked like very large peas in a pod.

Thebe pointed to the ten centimeter in diameter green peas, about the size of a grapefruit, and asked, "Shall we collect those?"

"They look promising," said Marcos. "But they are too high up."

"Climb on my shoulders," said Thebe.

Marcos climbed up and tried to reach in to pluck out one of the big round peas inside the plant. He wobbled a bit on Thebe's shoulders and pulled his arm back for balance. Just as he did, the 'mouth' of the plant snapped shut.

"What just happened?" asked Thebe.

Marcos stared at the plant as the mouth opened back up.

"The bad news is I didn't get the round part. The good news is I didn't lose my arm."

"Did you pack one of those extender grabby things in your backpack?"

"You mean a pick-up gripper?"

"That's probably a better name," said Thebe.

Marcos started to reach back to check his backpack but again started to wobble. Thebe quickly reached out to steady himself and grabbed a hold of the stalk of the flytrap. As soon as he put pressure on the stalk, the three 'peas' popped out and landed by Thebe's feet.

"Well that works," said Thebe.

Marcos jumped down.

They put the newly discovered peas in their backpacks.

Marcos said, "Hope these have some nutrients in them."

"Yeah, the last stuff we brought back was half seed and half shell."

"Hey, look over there. Is that a beach?"

"That must be where the stream runs to," speculated Thebe.

"Let's go check it out."

"Do we have time?"

"If we're fast, I think so."

As they walked past the plants, the plants drooped back down, and the roots leading to the beach shimmied up. Once they got to the beach area, they noticed that the roots went into the water.

Marcos reached into his backpack and pulled out a water-testing kit. "This water is salty."

"Try the water in the stream," suggested Thebe.

Marcos walked over to the end of the stream and tested the water. "It's not salty."

"This looks like a mangrove swamp back on Earth. With roots growing out of the salt water. The roots here seem to be avoiding the fresh water and seeking out the salt water."

"Except on Earth the mangrove trees don't have fruit."

Thebe said, "We'd better get back, it's been almost thirty minutes."

Marcos looked at the watch on the arm of his spacesuit, "You're right. Let's get going."

They started walking back quickly.

Marcos said, "If these have a good nutrient content, this will be a great crop to grow for people who live near the ocean and don't have good access to fresh water."

"My guess is that they are going to be very rich in nutrients, or they wouldn't have evolved such a strong defense to protect themselves," said Thebe.

They got back to the Quarker, hopped in, and buckled up.

"Ready?" asked Marcos.

"Ready," said Thebe.

Marcos pushed the button and they were back aboard the Space Zoo 1.

CHAPTER 52

Glenn, Sally, and their friends stood in front of their newly built crick pantry.

Janet, the Local News One reporter leaned over to the group and said, "Don't worry about a thing, this will be easy."

They all smiled nervously.

Janet looked at Glenn and asked, "Glenn, did you memorize the sheet that the Space Zoo Patrol sent to you?"

"Yes, ma'am."

"Good." She looked back at her videographer and asked, "Madelyn, are we ready?"

Madelyn said, "Yep," and flipped the switch which turned the camera on. Janet could hear the chatter from the studio in her earpiece. "…and the final word for the weather is sunny skies all weekend."

"Thanks Beth," said Jack, the news anchor. "Now out to the field for a special report."

Janet looked directly into the camera and started, "Thanks Jack. We're here today with a remarkable group of kids, Glenn, Sally, Mario, and Kali, who have just won a new award. Which one of you would like to tell our viewers about this prestigious award?"

Sally gave Glenn a little nudge so that he had to take a step forward.

"Ah, the spokesperson for the team. What's your name?"

"Glenn."

"Hello Glenn. What award did you just win?"

"It's the first annual National Society of Crick Collectors Golden Harvest Award."

"That sounds amazing. What does it mean?"

"We," Glenn said as he gestured to the group who waved and smiled, "just collected over 50,000 cricks."

"That's a lot of cricks. Normally families keep their cricks at their own house. Why are we here at this crick pantry at the Shepardville Park?"

"We have too many cricks and there wasn't enough room at each of our parents' homes. We had to make extra storage and this is a convenient location, here on Deke Drive, where we can get to it easily, especially by car."

"There you have it folks, an inspiration to us all. This is like a junior version of Fort Knox. Back to you in the studio."

The videographer turned the camera off.

Janet turned to the group, "Well done. That'll air tonight on the five o'clock, six o'clock, and seven o'clock news. Hopefully this broadcast will catch the attention of whoever has been stealing cricks in the area. I think the script was written in a way that will make these people feel the urgent need to come and check this out. Good luck guys."

"Thanks," they all said.

"Good job spokesperson," said Kali.

As the news crew was leaving, Janet turned and said, "And remember, don't get caught."

"I wish she hadn't said that," said Mario.

"We're not going to get caught," said Glenn to his friends. "Let's go home for dinner, then we'll meet at my house."

They all nodded, jumped on their bikes, and headed home, all of them hoping that this trap would work.

CHAPTER 53

After dinner the gang rode their bikes over to Glenn's house. He handed each one a tracker launcher. They all eagerly took one and looked at it, turned it over in their hands, and got a feel for it.

"It looks like a large TV remote," said Mario.

"How do they work?" asked Kali.

"I think you point it in the direction of the big yellow arrow," said Glenn.

There was a big yellow arrow at the top end of the device.

"And you push the big green button."

There was a big green button at the bottom end.

"I was joking" said Kali.

"Oh, sorry."

"No she wasn't," said Sally giving Kali a friendly poke.

"Everyone have their walkie talkies?" continued Glenn.

Everyone held up their walkie talkies.

"All right let's get going."

They all hopped on their bikes and rode a couple of blocks to the community storage shed.

"Let's hide behind the bushes over there," whispered Sally.

They all pulled their bikes behind a clump of bushes about twenty meters from the shed, and sat down, crouching, trying to stay out of sight.

All of a sudden, Mario jumped up and whispered, "I'll be right back. Stay hidden."

Everyone stared at him but he took off running.

A few seconds later he came back panting, "I went to the shed and looked to see if we could be seen. We're good."

Everyone looked relieved.

It was starting to get darker.

"How far will these things shoot?" asked Kali.

"I don't know," responded Glenn.

"What if they catch us?" asked Mario.

"They won't," Glenn, Sally, and Kali said at the same time.

"What if we all miss? Should we spread out?" asked Mario.

"Those are good questions," said Glenn.

"I have to go to the…" said Sally.

"Shhhh," everyone said, cutting her off.

After that, everyone was quiet. They kept looking at the shed periodically, and occasionally at their watches.

Now it was very late and very dark, and one by one they started to doze off.

All of a sudden they were jolted awake by the sound of a loud click. They very carefully peeked around the corner of the bushes and saw a large black truck. It had backed up to the shed. There was one person in the driver's seat, and a second person, at the shed door, was using bolt cutters to cut the lock. On his third try he was successful, and the door swung open. He put the cutters back in the truck and pulled out a large hose about thirty centimeters in diameter. He flicked a switch and pushed the end of the hose into the shed. The hose started sucking up the cricks making a soft crunching sound and shooting them into the truck. It looked like this had been an old county leaf collection truck and now they were using it to steal cricks.

After only a few seconds the theft was complete. The man stuffed the hose back into the truck and closed the back windowless doors. He then jumped back into the passenger seat of the truck.

The gang looked at each other in amazement.

"They're done already," Kali whispered quickly.

"They're starting to leave," said Mario. He sensed that he had to do something right away, and said, "I'm going to get their license number." He leaped out from behind the bushes and ran toward the truck. He tried not to be seen, and crouched as he ran, but the driver still saw him. The driver rolled his window down and yelled, "Hey you!" "That's not good," said Glenn.

Rather than panicking, Mario had another idea. Instead of turning around and heading back to the bushes which would have led the thieves to his friends, he ran in front of the truck. The truck started to go after him. Then Mario stopped, and the truck stopped to avoid hitting him. "This is our chance," said Glenn. When the truck stopped, it gave the rest of the gang enough time to maneuver behind the truck.

Once Mario saw his friends behind the truck, he ran down the road about ten meters, then stopped. The truck started chasing after him, but again, the driver had to slam his foot on the brakes and the truck screeched to a stop. The driver had no time to look in the rear view mirror.

Glenn, Sally, and Kali pulled out their trackers, took aim at the back of the truck, and fired. The shots were silent, and what came out looked like short blasts of clear Sticky String. The strings shot out very fast and looked like they could have gone one hundred meters in a straight line. All shots hit silently and stuck securely to the back doors.

Mario gave a quick look behind the truck and saw the gang giving him the thumbs up signal. Mario allowed himself a brief, tiny smile. He concentrated again on the driver, gave him a big grin, turned quickly, and sprinted down a jogging path between two big trees. He knew the truck could never follow him as the trees were too close together. "Don't mess with our cricks!" he shouted but kept running, just in case.

"I'm going to get him," the driver said, and started to open his door.

The gang took off running again at full speed back to the bushes. The driver never knew they were there.

"Let him go," said the thief in the passenger seat. "He's just a kid. How could he possibly hurt us?"

The driver angrily slammed his door closed, and pushed his foot down on the accelerator pedal.

As they drove off, the sticky strings inched up the back doors and onto the roof. The strings then started to glow a pale yellow and started to send out a tracking signal.

CHAPTER 54

It was early morning and several Space Zoo Patrol members were already on the bridge of Space Zoo 1. Some were working on computers, some were working on instruments that kept the space station circling in the right orbit. Jane sat at the main command seat on the bridge, partly working on the computer, partly watching the other members to see if any of them needed assistance, and partly looking at the beautiful Earth spinning below.

All of a sudden, a buzzer sounded. Jane looked at the computer screen and then looked serious. She pushed a button and the computer screens on the left combined to form one big screen. The screen showed a video download from a satellite. Everyone stopped what they were doing and looked up at the screen. The glowing tracking devices on the roof of the escaping truck had sent a signal to the satellite to start a tracking camera.

Jane spoke to the computer, "Overlay GPS map." Immediately a map showed up on the screen so they could see the street names of where the truck was going. The truck looked like it was traveling a little too fast. The Space Zoo Patrol had no way of knowing the driver was still angry and it was affecting his driving judgment. They did know that driving too fast was dangerous.

By now, Eddie and the interns, who had been working in their labs, had arrived on the bridge.

Back in the truck, the thief in the passenger seat was yelling at the driver, "Slow down, Dude. We shouldn't call attention to ourselves. Do you want to get caught speeding and have the police look in the back of the truck?"

The driver slowed down, "OK, OK. No one's going to catch us."

On the screen on the bridge, the Space Zoo Patrol saw that the truck slowed down a bit and was now traveling at a normal speed. The truck left the neighborhood and got on a freeway. It traveled for a few more minutes and then exited. It went into an old industrial area with buildings that were empty and falling down. The truck finally arrived at one building and pulled into a loading dock inside the building. Once inside, it could no longer be seen from the satellite. Still, everyone on the bridge continued to watch.

Portlay was at his desk watching his favorite TV channels and munching on potato chips, as usual. His phone rang and he leaned into the microphone attached to his chair and said, "Yes."
The driver of the truck carrying all the cricks said, "Hello, Sir. We've retrieved the cricks as you told us to do."
"Very good. You weren't followed were you?"
"No, we're OK. If you'll turn to your security monitor channel and check the incinerator outside of Shepardville you can watch our progress."
Portlay clicked some buttons and one of the screens showed the truck at the incinerator. This was an old county incinerator where they used to burn leaves before they realized that burning leaves put too much carbon dioxide into the air. Mega Global Food Corporation had bought up unused incinerators around the country to burn off food that was not in perfect condition, like when a

package was damaged during shipping. The food was still good inside but it would be difficult to sell at the store if a consumer thought it was bad. Food like this was supposed to go to homeless shelters, but Portlay didn't care. He destroyed the food thinking that if someone cared about feeding the homeless they would be forced to go to the store and buy new food. And of course Portlay's sales would go up and he would make more profit.

"I see you on screen. Go ahead."

The driver backed the truck up to a chute and pushed a button on the truck's dashboard. The back doors opened up automatically as the back portion of the truck tilted up. The cricks slid out into the chute. The driver quickly drove the truck forward a little as flames shot out of the chute. The driver pushed the button again and the back doors closed as the back of the truck lowered back into place.

"All done here, Sir," said the driver.

"Well done," said Portlay. He thought the driver probably wouldn't catch the cooking reference.

The driver turned off his phone and looked at the passenger and said, "Portlay just made another one of his lame cooking jokes."

A few minutes later, the Space Zoo Patrol could see on the screen smoke come pouring out of an old industrial chimney that was attached to the building.

Everyone on the bridge looked shocked and there were a few gasps.

"They're burning the cricks," said Marcos.

"You're recording this?" asked Eddie.

Jane gave a quick look at the green 'recording on' light, just to be sure it was on. "Yes," she said.

Jane turned to the interns and asked, "What do you think we should do next?"

They looked each other and shrugged.

Eddie looked at the interns and started to mouth an answer. "No helping," said Jane.

"We don't know, Sir," said John.

Jane leaned over to the computer and said, "Address."

1958 Eisenhower St., the address of the building where the truck had stopped, showed up on the screen.

"What's next?" Jane asked again.

The interns thought for a second. Then, John said, "I think we need to know who owns the building."

"Excellent," said Jane.

Jane leaned over the computer and said, "County records. Address ownership."

On the screen popped up *Mega Global Food Corporation.* John walked over to Jane's chair and spoke into the microphone, "Business records. Mega Global Food Corporation. Headquarters address."

On the screen popped up, *1930 Armstrong Avenue.*

John continued, "Mega Global Food Corporation. Ownership."

On the screen popped up, *Ian M. Portlay.*

Eddie said, "Good detective work. I think we need to pay Mr. Portlay a visit."

CHAPTER 55

During breakfast, all the interns were talking about the video of the truck that stole the cricks.

Eddie and Jane walked by and John asked a question, "Jane?"

"Yes," responded Jane.

"On the bridge, you asked us about how to catch the Mega Global Food Corporation truck. Those questions weren't about science. I thought we only had to know about science."

"We mostly study science up here," said Jane. "Science helps us figure out how things work and how we fit into this universe. The more science you know the better. However, the more you know about everything else, including history, literature, finance, government, business, and so on, the easier it is to understand where science fits into our lives and how science can help in those areas."

Eddie said, "Speaking of areas where we can help, we are going to give Mr. Portlay a visit later on today."

"Do we have time to go the gym?" asked Liz.

"Yes. Let's meet at the Zoomerang bay in two hours," said Eddie as he and Jane headed to the bridge.

CHAPTER 56

After breakfast, the interns walked down the hall to the gym. They learned in one of their briefings, when they first arrived on the Space Zoo One, that it is important to stay fit in space to counteract the negative aspects of zero gravity, mainly the loss of bone and muscle strength.

During the start of the space program, when astronauts returned to Earth, even after only three to four weeks, they had a hard time walking.

They entered the gym and they all got on the row of stationary bicycles and started pedaling slowly.

Marcos said, as he was peddling, "You know how the other day we all couldn't agree on the best type of pizza?"

Everyone nodded.

"I bet we can all agree on the best type of movie."

John said, "That's easy, it's historical dramas, they're real, nothing phony, plus they can be pretty inspirational."

Thebe said, "No way. It's action – adventure, especially in the jungle."

"I love romantic movies," said Liz.

"You're all wrong, it has to be comedy," said Marcos.

They looked at each other, realized they weren't going to agree on this either, and started pedaling furiously.

CHAPTER 57

After the interns finished at the gym, they showered, then went to the Zoomerang bay. Eddie entered the Zoomerang last and handed the pilot the Mega Global Food Corporation's address. After a smooth flight, the Zoomerang landed on the front lawn at the Mega Global Food headquarters. They got out of the Zoomerang, entered the main doors of the headquarters building, and walked up to the guard desk in the first floor lobby.

Eddie said, "Space Zoo Patrol here to see Mr. Portlay, please."

The guard had seen the Space Zoo Patrol on TV, but never in person. He stared at them as he fumbled for the phone. He called up to Portlay's office. As usual, Jim Slennar took the call.

"Hello Jim," said the guard, "the Space Zoo Patrol is here to see Mr. Portlay."

Jim Slennar knew of the Patrol's excellent reputation and said, "Send them up please."

The team went up the elevator and Jim saw them on the security monitor as they approached the main office. Slennar pushed a button and the doors opened automatically. Just as they were entering Portlay's office, Jim sneaked through the side door to the executive kitchen, and quietly closed the door behind him.

Portlay heard some noise and looked up. He was surprised that Slennar was gone but the team entered and he now focused on them.

"Ah, the illustrious Space Zoo Patrol. Welcome to my global headquarters. What can I do for you?"

"We'll get right to the point," said Eddie. "We have evidence that you are stealing cricks and destroying them.

People are having a hard time with less and less food. They don't need some unscrupulous business person stealing a food source just to increase his company's profits."

"Oh boo hoo. If these people think they can't afford my food, tell them to work harder. We have special lights added to our tractors so they can plow the fields even at night. My company provides more food than any company in history. If they think they are running out of food, tell them to stop having triple scoop ice cream cones. It's their fault not mine."

The team stared at Portlay who was holding a triple scoop ice cream cone in his hand.

Portlay scoffed, "This is just a snack to hold me over between breakfast and lunch. Plus, I can afford this."

"Yes, by doubling the price of food to everyone else," scolded Eddie

"I'm not breaking any laws."

"We think you are. We'll turn our videos of your people stealing cricks and burning them over to the police."

"I employ hundreds of thousands of people. I can't be responsible if one person does one little thing wrong."

"We think you should be. You direct this sort of thing to happen all the time."

"Send me a fine. I'll have one of my hundred accountants cut a check."

"Perhaps you should know that we will be introducing several new food sources. It's time that you had some competition. It's time that you lowered your prices so people can afford to eat."

"Get out, I'm busy," Portlay yelled as he took another bite of his ice cream.

Eddie looked at the interns and said, "I guess we won't be invited to their annual company picnic. Let's go."

The Space Zoo Patrol team turned, walked out through the office doors, and went to the elevators.

Portlay pushed a button on his chair and his office doors closed. He shouted, "Slennar, you coward. You can come out now."

Slennar came out from the kitchen.

"I'm not a coward. I thought if they hauled you away, someone would need to be here to run things."

"The chance of me being arrested is zero. The chance of you being able to run things here is zero. Now you listen to me. Find a way to get on their little space station, figure out what they meant by 'new food sources,' and put a stop to it."

As the Zoomerang departed, Jim sat at his desk to think of a way to get on the Space Zoo 1.

CHAPTER 58

The interns were having dinner in the cafeteria when Jane walked by, "Heard you had an interesting trip. How's everyone doing?"

"Fine, thank you," said Andy.

"We were just talking about how our goals are different than Mr. Portlay's," said Lu Lu.

"Well, if everybody does what they love, and they're good at it, and they don't get greedy, the long-term stuff seems to fall into place."

"What if you don't know yet what you love?" asked Thebe.

"Try as many things you can. You'll find something you really like."

"I want to make a difference," said John. "I want my hard work to mean something to others, not just myself. I don't want to just be a worker..."

Jane held a wing up to try to stop John in midsentence. But she was too late.

"...bee." Then said, "I'm sorry Sir, were you trying to stop me?"

"Yes."

"Why?" John asked.

They heard a faint buzzing sound in the distance, then it grew louder.

"You're about to find out. They have good hearing you know," said Jane.

About a hundred bees swarmed over to the table and looked at Jane. The lead bee moved a little closer to Jane.

Jane said to the interns, "They want to know who uttered the phrase 'worker bee.' "

John raised his flipper. The lead bee turned toward John and gave him a mean look.

Jane continued, "Bees work very hard to create honey, which we all enjoy, and they enjoy making it. They don't consider it work as they love what they do and would prefer not to be called worker bees."

John raised his eyebrows, looked at the bees, and said, "I'm sorry. I thought it was just an expression. I guess expressions can hurt. I won't use worker bee anymore."

It was hard to see exactly, but John thought he saw the lead bee nod just a little.

"Since you all love what you do, should we call you lover bees instead of worker bees?" asked John, with a smile.

The lead bee looked at John and gave him a little smile back.

Then the lead bee and the rest flew back to their hive in the honey room.

"Next time I have honey in my hot tea, I'll think of them and be a little more appreciative," said Liz.

CHAPTER 59

Several days later, Jim Slennar was at his desk still making phone calls. He then got up from his desk and was about to leave when Portlay looked at him.

"Where are you going?" asked Portlay.

"I figured out a way to get on the Space Zoo Patrol's space station."

"Good, good. How?"

"I contacted them, and they are sending one of their space shuttles to pick me up."

"And why would they do that?"

"I told them that you were sorry for your rudeness and I'm bringing them a delicious food gift basket as a way of saying that you apologize."

"They bought that? Who'd you talk with?"

"Oh, just some flunky."

"And then what?"

"Once I'm aboard the space station, I'll look around to find out what the new food source is and try to destroy it."

"Won't they notice you walking around?"

"I told them not to alert the main team that came down here. I wanted it to be a surprise."

"I love it. What are you waiting here for? Hurry up. Go, go, go."

CHAPTER 60

The Zoomerang docked onto the Space Zoo 1 without any problems. Jim Slennar handed the Commander of the shuttle a small fruit gift basket, "Thank you for a wonderful ride. Could you give me directions to the main area?"

"The bridge?" asked the Commander.

"Yes, that would be it."

"I'll show you."

"No, no. That's all right. I can make it by myself. I just need directions."

"OK. Turn right, go to the end of the hall, and take the elevator up to the bridge. But first, put on these visitors boots. They have magnets on the bottom. They'll keep you from floating away."

Jim slipped on the boots, thanked the pilot again, and left the docking bay. Once he was in the hallway, he looked for any signs on the walls showing directions to a laboratory or any place where they might be experimenting with new food sources. There was one sign that had an arrow to the bridge, an arrow to the cafeteria, and an arrow to the labs. He headed off to the labs. Once he was in the lab hall he saw several doors. He opened one, but there were no food items. He closed that door and went to the next one. Also empty. He went to several more doors, all empty until he came to the last one with the number 51 on it. He opened it. He walked in and Eddie, Jane, and all the interns were there.

"Mr. Slennar?" asked Eddie.

"Please, call me Jim."

"Welcome to the Space Zoo 1, we've been expecting you. Thanks for your call," said Jane. She then introduced all the interns.

Jim handed the large food basket to Eddie.

"Thank you," said Eddie.

All the interns reached in to grab a piece of fruit or a piece of cake.

Jim grew up in a good home and had gone to good schools, so he said gently to the interns, "As you probably know, it is proper etiquette to open the card first before you open the gift."

The interns backed away and looked apologetic.

Jim continued, "The gift basket is from Mr. Portlay. The card is from me."

The interns looked puzzled. Eddie and Jane smiled. Eddie then opened the envelope. There was no card, but there was a thumb drive.

Eddie held it up, "Thank you again."

"Every financial transaction Portlay has made in the last ten years is on that," said Jim. "Every pay-off, every bribe, every check to the people who picketed a store to make the owner sell."

The interns all cheered and clapped.

"This is fabulous," said Jane. "This ought to help put him away for years. I wonder how he'll like prison food?"

Everyone laughed.

"Let's take Jim to the bridge so he can get a special Space Zoo Patrol view of the world he has just helped."

"Wait," said Marcos. "I have an important question."

"Yes," said Eddie.

"Now can we have some cake?"

Jane said, "You all stay here and eat as much as you want. We'll take Mr. Slennar to the bridge.

A few minutes later, Jim Slennar was on the bridge staring out of the main windows. "This is amazing," he said.

Jane nodded to Eddie. Eddie looked at Jim and said, "We have to set up a company to manage and distribute all the new food we'll be growing. We really don't know anything about that. We hope that you would be interested in being president of the new company."

Slennar looked stunned, then pleased. With a big smile he said, "Yes, of course. Thank you. I'd be delighted." He paused, looked out of the windows for a moment, then continued, "But only if I get to bring food gift baskets up here periodically."

"Deal," said Eddie.

CHAPTER 61

The next day, Marcos, Thebe, and Lu Lu decided to go on another expedition. They landed on the Exo 1.

Thebe opened the door, looked out, and slammed the door shut quickly. "We have to leave right away," he said.

"What's wrong?" asked Lu Lu.

"We're in a 'No Parking' zone," responded Thebe with a straight face as he winked at Marcos.

Marcos laughed and so did Thebe.

Lu Lu then laughed too. "You had me worried for a minute."

"OK, let's go," said Marcos.

Thebe opened the door and stepped out. All they heard was a loud 'squoosh.' Thebe sunk in and all they could see from within the Quarker was the back of Thebe's head.

"Hey, stop kidding around," said Lu Lu.

"I'm not kidding. Take a look," said Thebe.

Lu Lu and Marcos peered out of the door.

"Are you all right?" she asked.

"I'm OK, but the quote 'One small step for mankind, one giant squoosh for Thebe,' isn't going in the history books."

"What's it like out there?" asked Marcos.

"A little soft. Kind of spongy."

"Should we use the jet boots?" asked Lu Lu.

"I didn't bring any. Did you?" asked Thebe.

Both Marcos and Lu Lu said, "No."

"I like the idea of walking on the ground anyway. I think we see more. But we need to make something like snowshoes. What do you see inside the cabin that we could use?" asked Thebe.

"The interior is covered with plastic panels," said Marcos as he looked around. He tried to pop one loose and it popped right off.

Lu Lu said, "Look, behind you. There's a panel that says 'Emergency Tools.' "

Marcos opened it. There were wrenches, a screwdriver, and a roll of duct tape.

"Perfect," said Marcos. "Come back in."

Thebe climbed back in and they quickly pulled off five more panels. Then they taped on their make-shift 'sponge-shoes' and headed out.

CHAPTER 62

Eddie and Jane were sitting in chairs in Lab 51 to talk in private.
"Marcos, Thebe, and Lu Lu are still on Exo 1," said Eddie, quietly.
"I know. They should be back by now," said Jane, also sounding worried.
"I'm sure they're OK." said Eddie, trying to sound upbeat.

However, on Exo 1, a herd of giant snails were getting closer to Marcos, Thebe, and Lu Lu.

"I thought we established some rules for how long they could stay out. We told them the maximum time was thirty minutes. How long do you think they've been gone?" asked Jane.
"About forty minutes."
"What if they stay too long? What happens then?"
"Yelie's research indicated they would make it back."
Yelie's lights blinked on when she heard her name.
"Yelie. What's the longest that you stayed on Exo 1?" asked Jane.
"One hundred eighteen minutes. And with no snacks on the flight I might add."
"Thank you Yelie. What if they are in trouble?"
"I don't know," responded Eddie.
"You find that acceptable?"
"No."
"You seem pretty calm," noted Jane.
"I'm trying to think of a plan."
"For the problem right now or for the long-term question of how long to stay out?"

"To solve the long-term problem. It has bigger consequences."

"Bigger consequences? You think the interns are expendable? You think they're lab rats?"

A group of lab rats in a nearby test maze stood on their hind legs, each held up a paw, and were about to say something...

Jane held up a wing, gave them a stern look, and said, "Not now." She looked at Eddie then back at the rats and said, "I get it. Sorry."

The lab rats settled down and went back to timing each other in the maze.

Jane looked back at Eddie, raised her eyebrows, and cocked her head side to side, as if to say 'I need answers.'

Eddie smiled a little and said, "Not to worry. I may have a short-term solution." He pulled out his phone, pushed a few buttons, then said, "We need your help. Can you meet us in Lab 51?"

He listened, then said, "Thanks." He turned back to Jane and said, "The cavalry will be here in a minute."

And less than a minute later, the two Retrievers bounded into the lab, their tails wagging.

Eddie looked directly at them in a serious manner waiting for their tails to stop wagging. As soon as they did he said, "During World War II, General George Marshall said, 'I want an officer for a secret and dangerous mission. I want a West Point football player!' " Eddie paused for a second, then continued, "We need someone for a dangerous mission. We need a member of the Space Zoo Patrol."

The two Retrievers looked at each other, then Dave said, "We're in."

"How's your sense of smell?" asked Jane.

Paul smiled and said, "The average human has five million smell receptors…dogs have anywhere from 125 million to 300 million."

Dave added, "Plus, during school, we interned with the FBI, and we learned to smell out evidence no matter how well hidden it is. One time, a bad guy tried to hide a piece of evidence in a plastic bag, inside a welded steel container filled with gas."

"Boom," said Paul as he pumped his paw, "smelled it and caught the creep." Both tails wagged.

"First," said Jane, "wow, that's amazing. Second, never say boom in a space station."

The Retrievers nodded. "What do you want us to do?" asked Dave.

"Track three missing interns on the exoplanet," said Eddie. Both tails stopped wagging.

Everyone was quiet for a few seconds.

The Retrievers looked at each other, then Dave said, "Anything for our teammates."

"Whooo," Jane let out a sigh of relief.

Eddie said, "Excellent."

Both tails wagged again.

Eddie pulled the tarp off of Quarker 2 and pointed to a closet with jet boots. "You guys grab the jet boots they left behind, they may need them. There are more for you in Quarker 2. I'll input the coordinates for your trip, plus our return coordinates."

Eddie input the coordinates and the Retrievers climbed into Quarker 2. Eddie asked, "Do you need something of theirs to smell?"

"No thanks," said Dave.

"We bunk with them, we eat with them, we study and exercise with them. We know what they smell like," said Paul.

"Is Thebe one of the missing interns?" asked Dave.

"Yes," answered Jane. "Why?"

"He took a mud bath this morning. We'll find them."

"OK. When the door is locked and your seatbelts are on, then push the green button."

Jane started to wave, but poof, Quarker 2 was gone.

CHAPTER 63

Quarker 2 landed on Exo 1 and the Retrievers opened the
door. They cautiously put a paw out and felt that the ground
was too soft to support them. They put on their jet boots,
put the spare jet boots in their back packs, and got out.
They hovered just off the ground and started sniffing for
their friends. They caught a scent and moved off to the
right.

They traveled about half a kilometer and then spotted
Quarker 1. Dave hovered closer and looked inside,
"They're not inside. But some panels are missing."
Paul, hovering above asked, "Are the panels square?"
"Yes."
"I see a path. They aren't footprints. The path was created
by square objects. This must be them."
Dave said, "Good, let's follow the path."
They followed the 'sponge shoe' prints. The distance
between the prints looked fairly uniform, like they were
walking at a slow deliberate pace. Obviously they were
taking their time searching for the right food. Then the
Retrievers saw more than a dozen large slick paths leading
to and following the interns' path. The prints now looked
to be farther apart, like they were trying to run.
Dave said, "They might be in trouble. Let's hurry."
They leaned forward and pushed a button on their arm
control unit to speed up.
After about a kilometer they saw the interns huddled
together, trapped by a cliff on one side and several giant
snails closing in on them from the other side.
The snails were the size of elephants with three horns on
their heads like a Triceratops.

"Those are some of the scariest animals I've ever seen," said Dave.

The retrievers dropped down and handed the other interns their jet boots.

They took off their make-shift sponge shoes, and put on their jet boots. They tossed the door panels into their backpacks, and blasted off. They escaped just as the snails were getting to them.

Marcos looked back as they jetted off and a snail turned its head to look up. What Marcos saw amazed him. He saw a tear in the snail's eye. He turned back.

Everyone else yelled at him to keep going.

Thebe yelled, "What are you doing?"

Lu Lu yelled, "Come on!"

Marcos landed in front of the lead snail.

The snail's tears stopped and it smiled.

Marcos held his paw out. The snail leaned its head down and licked his paw. Marcos petted the snail's head and said, "Hello big fella. I'd love to stay, but we have to go. See you next time."

The snail looked up with a big smile.

Marcos jetted off and joined the others who had been hovering and staring in amazement.

Everyone was too stunned to say a word.

They got back to Quarker 1, the original trio of interns climbed in, and pushed the green button. The Retrievers got back to Quarker 2 where they repeated the same procedure. Quarker 1 returned safely to Space Zoo 1, and they all climbed out.

Quarker 2 arrived and the Retrievers jumped out.

"Thank you," said Lu Lu, Thebe, and Marcos enthusiastically.

"Glad you're safe," said Dave.

Lu Lu said to Marcos, "You should wash your paw with soap and water."

"Nah," said Marcos. "I'm the first living being to be licked by an exoplanet snail. Let's see if I get an allergic reaction."

"I got photos. Let's go show the others," said Thebe.

"Let's go show Eddie and Jane first. They'll want to see that you're safe," said Paul.

They nodded and headed to the bridge.

CHAPTER 64

Eddie and Jane had been waiting anxiously on the bridge.
Lu Lu called the other interns to let them know they had
returned and were heading to the bridge. They all arrived
together.

Eddie and Jane looked relieved.

"Thanks for sending the Retrievers' to retrieve us," said
Marcos.

"That's what we do," said Dave.

Eddie smiled, "I'm glad you're back. What was the
holdup? Wait, before you answer…" he looked at Thebe.
"What's on your face?"

Thebe moved over to look in a mirror and saw some green
slime on his face. "Oh, I must have sunk in farther than I
thought. The ground was really soft."

"Did you inhale any or did any get in your mouth?" Eddie
asked urgently.

"I don't think so."

"Let's be safe and get you to sickbay for some quick tests."

"I'm fine."

Eddie looks sternly at Thebe, "That's the exact line
everyone says right before they get sick."

Marcos said, "Come on, we'll walk with you."

As they turned to leave the bridge, Marcos said, "Maybe
they should look at the back of my hand too."

Eddie said, "OK, now I'm really curious."

"Oh, I think it's a good thing," said Marcos.

Along the way Thebe, Marcos, and Lu Lu described their
trip and showed Eddie the pictures. Eddie was amazed.
When they got to sickbay, Thebe stepped into the Medical
Inspection Unit, labeled MIU. It was like an open closet
but it had all sorts of medical instruments attached inside.

The automated system put Thebe through the usual battery of tests: temperature, blood pressure, inspect the throat, plus a new test where it scanned the blood from the outside without having to draw blood. The automated voice said, "Patient is in good health."

"I think the doctor means I'm fine," said Thebe as he stepped out of the MIU.

"I am delighted to hear it," said Eddie.

Marcos placed his paw into the unit. A device scanned his paw. The voice said, "Patient has no contagions."

"What's neat," said Marcos, "is that I had a small cut on my paw from working on the robot the other day, and it's now completely healed."

"Doctors on Earth now routinely use leeches and maggots to help heal patients. Your snail friend has an even greater potential to help. You'll have to go back and collect a sample of his saliva. Then we, hopefully, can duplicate it, and make an ointment for use on Earth."

"He seemed pretty nice. I think he would let me take a sample. Then maybe he'll let me climb on and take me for a ride."

"Maybe we can all go back and have snail races," said Lu Lu, only half-jokingly.

CHAPTER 65

It was late at night and everyone had turned in for the evening. All was peaceful on the bridge. There were just a few junior officers there, watching the gauges and keeping track of things to make sure the space station was safe. All of a sudden, the buzzer went off and the red warning lights started flashing. This time the buzzer was loud and the flashing lights were very bright. This was no drill, it was obviously an emergency.

Chris was in charge when the alarm sounded. He spoke into the microphone and said, "Solar system map on screen." All the small screens merged into one large screen to show the large map of Earth's solar system. "Overlay warning system grid."

On the screen came a grid of hundreds of little red dots indicating sensors that were placed in the solar system to indicate any motion that went undetected by the major telescopes. This system was much like the system of buoys in the ocean to detect tsunamis. Some of the red dots started blinking.

"Extrapolate." Extrapolate meant to project a future outcome based on the current data, in this case, the few existing dots that were blinking. Much like if somebody said one, two, three, you could guess the next number they would say would be four. Or if someone in a car with a surfboard on top said 'I'm in Boston, Massachusetts' and then said 'Now I'm in Washington, DC' and then said 'I'm in Savannah, Georgia.' you could guess that they were heading to Cocoa Beach, Florida to go surfing. In this case the computer extended the line from one dot to the next and the next and then made a calculation that extended the line.

The red line showed that whatever was causing the sensors to go off, was heading straight towards Space Zoo 1!
Chris looked frightened, he leaned over to the microphone and started to talk but all that came out was a frightened "Honk." It was the loudest goose honk anyone on the bridge had heard in a long time. Chris shook his head, rubbed his throat, and said, "Sorry." He leaned back over the microphone and said, "Jane to the bridge. Emergency." Jane showed up in less than a minute wearing bright pink pajamas. Everyone looked at Jane. "What? You said emergency."
Chris pointed at the map, "Look."
Jane looked at the map, "I hope we have time." She jumped into her command seat, leaned over the microphone, and said, "Command Authorization Code 10.1.58." The computer screen flashed the words 'Command Authorization Accepted.' Jane started to push some buttons on her computer, and the normally quiet Space Zoo 1 started to hum as thruster engines turned on. Slowly, but surely the massive space station stated to move.
The line on the screen was getting closer.
By now, Eddie and all the interns were on the bridge. Everyone looked at Jane.
Jane said to the interns, "If we kept the station in its current orbit we would risk being hit by whatever is heading our way. If we move any closer to Earth, the station risks being drawn into Earth's gravitational field. So the only maneuver left was to push farther out into space. However, if we move too far we would use all our fuel and wouldn't have enough left to stop the station and we could keep drifting out into space forever."

Jane pushed some more buttons, then spoke to the interns without looking up, "This is tricky, I have to account for yaw, pitch, and roll, adjustments. I have to get it moving without making it tumble. In airplane maneuvering lingo, yaw means side-to-side, pitch means the nose going up and down, and roll means spiraling like a football. The International Space Station weighs 419,000 kilograms and the Space Zoo 1 is at least triple that. Even in space this takes a lot of engine power to get it to move."

The thrusters rumbled some more and everyone could feel the station shudder a bit.

"Is anything going to snap off?" asked Lu Lu.

"No. We're solid," said Eddie.

The station stated to move.

The map showed the object getting closer.

The station was now moving slowly.

More red lights blinked on the map.

Jane pushed some more buttons. The three Zoomerangs that were docked, now moved out of their bays and remotely moved to the side of the space station. The three ships just touched their noses to a solid portion of the station and their thrusters came on. The Space Zoo 1 moved a little faster.

Eddie looked at Chris, and said, "See if you can synch the sensor readings into the long range telescope. Let's try to see this thing."

Chris leaned over the computer console and typed in some commands.

The big screen changed over to a scene of black space with a blurry dot in the middle. The telescope adjusted and the object came more into focus.

"It's a comet," said Eddie.

"How can you tell?" asked John.

"It's got a glow to it. The sun is reflecting off the ice. If it was an asteroid, a rock, it wouldn't be reflective and it would be hard to see."

Everyone held their breath for the next few minutes.

The comet passed by. It was a spectacular sight with the ice and rock head and long tail shimmering in the sunlight.

And then it was gone.

Everyone breathed a sigh of relief, applauded Jane, and gave each other high-fives.

Someone called out from the back, "Good job, Jane. Way to go."

Eddie walked over and patted her on the back and said, "Thank you. Well done." Then he looked around the room, "I don't know what was brighter, the comet or Jane's pajamas."

Everyone laughed.

"Just doing my job," said Jane. "Everyone can go back to bed. I'll bring us back to our original orbit. Everything's fine."

Jane reached over to the computer console and pushed a few buttons and all the lights on the bridge went out.

A second later the emergency battery power kicked in and a few small lights came back on.

Everyone looked a little nervous and started talking to each other.

"I've never seen this before," said Chris. "I hope we can fix this."

"Did we use up all the fuel moving to a higher orbit?" asked Andy.

"No," said Jane. "We have enough to get back to our normal orbit. All the electrical equipment is run off the solar panels, and they weren't hit."

"With all the movement, are the panels still facing the sun?" asked Thebe.

Everyone looked out the main windows and could see the panels were still correctly oriented toward the sun.

Eddie walked over to the main window for a better look. "They're not shiny," he said.

"They're covered in microscopic rock and ice dust from the tail of the comet."

"How are we going to clean that off?" asked Chris.

"I don't know," said Eddie. "The solar panels have no moving parts, they never need maintenance, they always work." He thought for a minute. He could tell everyone was looking at him. "We can't hose them off, the water pressure might hurt them. The solar panels on Earth are sturdier and can be hosed off. These are very thin and lightweight to make them easier to launch into space."

Eddie glanced around the room, as if looking for inspiration. He looked at the two Retrievers and said, "I have an idea."

A few minutes later, down at the airlocks, Eddie looked at the two Retrievers, who were now in their full space suits. "You know what to do."

The Retrievers nodded, then opened the inner airlock door and stepped in. Eddie closed the inner door then the Retrievers opened the outer door. They used their jetpacks to float out of the space station, then they carefully maneuvered over to the solar panels. They turned their backs to the solar panels and faced the main windows. They could see everyone on the inside, now all pressed up against the windows. Everyone, the officers, the junior officers, and the interns were all waving and smiling. The Retrievers were as happy as could be, and naturally started to wag their tails. The sections of their spacesuits that covered their tails were now covered in goose feathers, held on by duct tape. Their tails swept back and forth, like giant feather dusters, gently across the solar panels. The comet dust started to float away.

"It's working," announced Eddie.

Everyone cheered except Chris and Berty. They gently massaged their bottoms, which were now missing a few tail feathers.

The Retrievers used their jetpacks to maneuver along the entire length of the solar panels, and soon, all the panels were clean.

Jane went back to the command chair and pushed a button. All the lights and computer screens came back on and everyone cheered again. Jane leaned over to the microphone and said, "Excellent work you two! Come on back inside."

CHAPTER 66

Everyone slept in late the next day after being up for much of the night with the comet scare.

After brunch, Eddie came over to the interns' table and said, "Ready to go pay a last visit to Mr. Portlay?"

Everyone nodded sleepily.

"Meet you at the Zoomerang bay in ten minutes."

The Zoomerang landed at the Mega Global Food Corporation headquarters and they were greeted by the local police officer, who they had called earlier. They all went into the lobby and the front desk guard had the elevator ready for them. They got to the top floor and the police officer knocked on the door. They heard Portlay scream for Slennar who was not there. The police officer said, "Open the door, it's the police."

The door opened. Portlay was at his desk.

The officer walked in first, followed by the Space Zoo Patrol. "Mr. Portlay, we have a warrant for your arrest."

Portlay stared at the officer, then stared at Eddie. "You," he said in a snarling tone. "This is all your fault. You guys think you're so cool floating around in space. What's space exploration done for me lately?"

Eddie smiled, "You mean besides satellite communications for TVs, cell phones, and GPS systems? Doppler radar for early severe weather warning?"

Portlay shook his head, indicating he didn't care.

Eddie continued, "Water purification systems? LED lights? Smoke detectors? Flat panel TV's? Solar energy? Breast cancer detection?"

Portlay uttered two words, "Big deal."

"Shock absorbers for buildings and bridges to keep them safe during earthquakes? Memory foam?

"Nope."

"Putting men on the moon?"

"Nope."

"Tell him something he'll understand. You know the one," said Marcos.

"Well it's just not that big a deal anymore."

"Try it anyway."

"TANG."

"I love TANG!"

"All right, that's enough," said the officer. "You're going to jail, pal. Plus, I'm giving you a ticket for being unappreciative of an amazing space program."

The officer wheeled Portlay out to a waiting reinforced patrol wagon.

Eddie and the interns hopped back aboard their Zoomerang.

CHAPTER 67

It had been an eventful day watching Portlay's empire built
on greed come crashing down.

After a relaxing dinner, Jane walked the group of interns to
the Core, then down a hall, and finally to a storage room
that had various boxes strapped to the walls and floor.

"Everyone in? I know it's cramped. OK, good, we're all
here. I hope you've been comfortable in your sleeping
quarters in the Wheel, which, as you know, provides you
with a sense of gravity. However, periodically we practice
sleeping in a zero gravity environment."

"Why?" asked Lu Lu. "I like the regular way of sleeping."
Several others nodded in agreement.

"Me too," said Jane. "But there will be many times in your
space careers that you will be in a weightless environment
and it will be helpful to become familiar with the essentials
of your weightless sleep compartment. So, everyone, take
off your gravity boots, and float to the nearest sleep
compartment."

Everyone took off their boots and grabbed a pipe or box
and pushed off. It didn't take much effort to float free.
They all looked around and found an assortment of webbed
or solid cloth compartments attached to the walls. Some
were vertical, some were horizontal, depending on the
availability of an open spot on the wall.

"Some of you will like a webbed compartment, so you can
see around the room, some of you will prefer an enclosed
compartment so you won't be bothered by any movement
around the room. Whichever one you try this time, try the
other version next time."

Everyone found a compartment to their liking.

"OK. Slide in. Now zip the material to form a door, just like in a tent. That way you won't float away in the night." Everyone zippered in.

"There are straps inside the compartment in case you want to feel more snugged in place, up to you. In here, there is no up or down. There is no need for a pillow. Yes, it feels awkward at first. That is why we have these practice sessions, so that when you are on a mission in a ship with no artificial gravity, you can get to sleep quickly and not let it interfere with your work schedule. So, sleep tight and see you in the morning."

Jane turned out the lights and left the room.

"How can you sleep tight if you are floating in space?" asked Thebe.

"It's just an old Earth expression. Try the straps, they help," suggested Andy.

At first everyone was still wide-eyed, finding getting to sleep indeed awkward. But, eventually, they all dozed off. After a while, Marcos's wristwatch alarm, set to vibrate, went off. He woke up, quietly unzipped his compartment door, and floated out. He floated over to Thebe. He tapped Thebe, and when Thebe woke up, Marcos put his finger to his lips to indicate no talking. He motioned for Thebe to follow him. Thebe unzipped his compartment and floated out.

Marcos went to Lu Lu's compartment, unzipped her door, gently tugged on her suit, freed her of her sleeping compartment and let her quietly float around the room.

He motioned for Thebe to do the same. They undid all the other compartments, and one by one, all the others were sleep-floating around the room too.

Marcos and Thebe went back to their compartments and had a good night's sleep.

They awoke the next morning to several annoyed shouts of "Marcoooos!" and "Theeeebe!"

CHAPTER 68

On the ride back from Portlay's office in the Zoomerang, Eddie had told the interns to finalize their research and be ready to give their presentations. Today was the day, and they all met in the conference room.

This time the interns stood at the front of the room and Eddie and Jane sat at the back, along with their guest, Jim Slennar.

Jane started off the meeting, "Some time ago, we all embarked on a major project, namely to help get more food for the planet. You have all been to the exoplanet to find new food. In addition we asked you to do some research into other areas that may be of help. Please tell us your findings."

Thebe and Marcos went first. They had just finished their research on the big green 'peas' they found and were eager to tell everyone what they found.

Thebe started, "On one of our trips to the exoplanet we stumbled across these large round vegetables hiding inside a flytrap type plant. At first we thought they were fruit, but they turned out to be more like chickpeas or garbanzo beans. So this vegetable, which according to our analysis is very high in both carbohydrates and protein would be a good source of food. We found that the roots of the plant were being fed by salt water. So we realized that this would be a perfect plant for people who live near salt water and don't have much access to fresh water. Which is a lot of people."

Marcos stepped forward, "We wanted to see if we could grow them here using our hydroponic system but adding salt water. We knew a few things from one of our first lab experiments on tomatoes and hydroponics. But we did a little more research. We found that hydroponics were first used in Babylon over two thousand years ago. The famous Hanging Gardens of Babylon were made with stone and mud bricks. Their system wasn't used after the gardens were destroyed a century later. The system really became workable after light-weight plastic PVC piping became readily available in the 1950s. The PVC system is inexpensive, lightweight, and readily available. So, this system could be built easily by many people. For example, people who live in the city should set up roof-top hydroponic gardens. For our plants, we researched the proper temperature, the correct levels of salt and water, and the right lighting. Since these vegetables have no seeds we cut them up into pieces just as if you were planting potatoes."

Thebe added, "As you see," a picture of the roots appeared on the screen, "the roots are coming along nicely. Another benefit to this plant is that you don't need to add any salt during cooking or at the table, as it already has plenty from the salt water."

"Oh," said Marcos, "there is a little trick to gathering the peas. You just have to give a tap on the stalk, you don't have to stick your arm into the trap portion."

"Well done," said Eddie. "Any questions from the group?" No one had any questions. They were all busy eating the sample peas.

Jane smiled and added, "That was a good report. Once we get more, we'll ship them down to Earth."

Jim added, "We can call them 'flytrap peas.' The public might find that name 'catchy.' "

Everyone groaned.

Lu Lu and John were up next.

"Lu Lu and John, we understand you have an amazing new idea," said Jane.

Lu Lu said, "Thank you. Yes, we think we have a way to help grow more crops. We found out there was so much land that used to have soil but it has eroded away and can no longer be used as farm land. The soil was eroded by both wind and rain and now is just down to bedrock. Just in the United States alone, there are 544 million metric tons of soil eroded each year. We figured out a way to replace that soil."

John continued, "There are 100 million metric tons of sewage, 208 million metric tons of food waste, and 31 million metric tons of yard waste produced each year in the United States. We propose that someone should collect all 339 million tons and compost it. Composting reduces the water and so you are left with about half of the original amount, in this case 170 million tons of new soil. That will help a lot."

"What about germs?" asked Eddie.

"The heat from the composting process is enough to kill any germs," pointed out Lu Lu.

"This is exciting," said Jane.

"I hope we can convince the governments to spend the extra money to collect all the waste material," said Jim.

"If it will help feed people, why wouldn't they?" asked John.

"You'd be surprised at what they will spend money on and what they won't spend money on," said Jim rather glumly.

Andy and Liz were next, and they stepped forward.

Andy stated, "Our research showed that one way to need less food to begin with is to reduce food waste.

Approximately thirty-one percent of all food grown and delivered to grocery stores, restaurants, and homes goes uneaten and is tossed out. This is a huge and terrible waste."

Liz said, "In the home, every family should use plastic food storage containers. The airtight seal keeps air, and the bacteria in the air, out of the container and the food. This helps food last longer."

Andy added, "Both grocery stores and families should buy local fruits and vegetables as they travel a shorter distance and less goes to waste than when food travels long distances in trucks. People with yards should grow their favorite vegetable at home."

Liz said, "Grocery stores and restaurants should pay more attention to the amount that they purchase so they don't throw out as much."

Andy said, "And finally, restaurants should collect the food that has been untouched and deliver it to food kitchens for the hungry. This food may be irradiated with gamma rays or x-rays which kill harmful bacteria but passes right through the food."

"Great presentation," said Jane.

"Thank you interns," said Eddie. "These are all excellent suggestions. We will make sure your recommendations get to the proper government officials."

In the meantime, "Let's go have lunch. Mr. Slennar will join us as our guest."

Jim said, "Here's an old saying that applies to eating your meal, 'Take what you want, but eat what you take.' I look forward to talking with you at lunch. In addition, I brought up some special desserts for you."

The interns cheered.

CHAPTER 69

After lunch with the special desserts, the interns went to the gym to work off the extra calories. Then they went to the bridge to join the rest of the crew and watch a major sporting event on the big screen.

It was Saturday afternoon in Shepardville, and Glenn's school was playing a nearby school in the local kickball tournament. It wasn't being broadcast by any sports channel, but it was a major sporting event in Shepardville. Everyone on the field was excited and everyone on the bridge was excited.

Both teams played well for several innings. Now it was the bottom of the last inning and the score was tied 5 – 5. Two outs, and the bases were loaded. Glenn was up. He looked at Mario and said, "I've got to do something different. I got thrown out the last two times."

"You kick it flat, soccer style. The ball just doesn't go far enough. Look, the other team's infield is playing you in. You need to kick it over their heads."

Kali said, "You're good at math, just change the angle."

Glenn nodded, "I need to change the angle of my kick. I'll change my kick to football style."

Glenn walked over to home plate, the ball was pitched, and he gave it a huge, football-style, kick. The ball sailed over the infielders' heads and his teammate on third ran home to score.

Glenn's teammates cheered wildly.

Glenn stood on first base and smiled. He then looked up to see the small yellow video drone hovering about one hundred meters above the field. He gave it a thumbs up. Back up in the Space Zoo 1 everyone on the bridge cheered wildly, too.

CHAPTER 70

Later that day, Andy and Liz landed on Exo 1. They got out, opened their laptop, opened the box that contained the drone with the ground penetrating radar, and guided it upward.

On their screen they saw beautiful countryside from the aerial photography.

After a few minutes, Andy said, "That ought to do it for the geographic mapping."

Liz said, "OK, let's switch over to GPR for the geological mapping."

After a while, Liz noticed something on the screen. "Do you see this?"

Andy looked more closely, "Is that supposed to move?"

"I thought the lines might be different from one area to the next, but the lines should be the same lines every time the drone sweeps over the same area. I have sent it over that area over there several times and each time the pulses rebound differently."

Andy was puzzled too. "Much of the ground under the surface on this planet is saturated with water, which may be why everything here grows so well. Maybe there are underground waves. Slower than we are used to in our oceans above the ground, but maybe waves just the same."

"That would be interesting," said Liz. "Oop…Did you feel that?"

"Yes, a little."

"Do you think the GPR is causing the waves?"

"Maybe. Turn it off."

Liz pushed the button. The drone kept circling, but with no GPR pulses.

"I don't feel anything," said Andy. "Turn it on again."

Liz turned the GPR back on, and immediately the ground vibrated again. This time the vibrations were stronger.

"I definitely felt that," said Andy.

Then there was a groaning sound.

"I definitely heard that," said Liz.

Then, a massive worm wriggled out from under the ground. It was about five meters in diameter and about fifty meters long.

"I definitely see that," said Liz. She pointed to the area where the drone was flying over.

"Maybe that's another reason why the soil is so rich here. Just like on Earth, worms make the soil richer by composting dead material and mixing up the dirt."

"It's coming at us. Maybe the pulses woke him up. Let's discuss this later," said Liz.

"Bring down the drone," said Andy.

Liz signaled for it to hover down. They packed up the drone and laptop and ran to the Quarker.

They both shouted, "Door open!" They hopped in and closed the door just as the worm opened its mouth and swallowed the Quarker.

They hadn't had time to put on their seatbelts and so were tossed around inside the Quarker. Andy grabbed ahold of a seat, lunged to the console, and pushed the green button. Poof. They were back in Lab 51.

"Well, this will make an interesting report," said Liz.

"Yeah. This guy didn't want to lick our paws," said Andy.

CHAPTER 71

After dinner, Eddie and Jane sat in their command chairs staring out of the main windows, discussing the following day's graduation ceremony for the interns.

Jane said, "An excellent graduating class this year."

Eddie, with a big grin said, "Yes. They studied well. I'm proud of all of them."

Outside the front window, crossing over the normally peaceful view of the spinning Earth, a tennis ball flew by, then Dave, in his space suit, chased it using his jetpack. He caught it, then threw it back to Paul, who chased it down. This continued for some time.

Jane sighed, "All of them?"

Eddie, after a pause, said, "Yeah…all of them."

CHAPTER 72

The next morning, the bridge looked a little more festive than usual. It was the day of the interns' graduation ceremony, and there were balloons and crepe streamers. Of course the balloons didn't float up, they kind of floated around, and the crepe streamers didn't drape down they were taped in place. But it added a little bit of fun to the place.

The bridge was packed, almost every Space Zoo Patrol member was there. A few couldn't come as they were monitoring the engine room or monitoring lab experiments. Everyone who was there, was standing with their backs to the main windows and faced the command chairs. The interns were front and center.

Eddie and Jane were the last to arrive. They walked in from the back doors, went straight to the command chairs, and continued standing.

Eddie raised his paws slightly as a signal for everyone to stop talking. As soon as the room quieted down, Eddie spoke up. He looked out over the crowd, "Thank you all for coming. We are here today to celebrate the graduation of our recent group of interns." He looked down at the interns and gave a big smile.

Jane also smiled and said, "And they are graduating because of their many accomplishments."

There was a smattering of applause from the crowd.

Jane, looked at the interns, "You've shown exceptional skills in each of the six major areas of science.

In astronomy, you helped find new planets.

In biology, you helped expand our hydroponics program and discovered new food on the exoplanet.

In chemistry, you helped determine a new formula to help cure cuts.

In geology, you helped map a new planet using ground penetrating radar.

In math, you used equations to help determine the number of drones you would use for the hurricane destabilization project.

In physics, you helped determine how to destabilize the hurricanes.

And, in addition to your scientific skills, you showed bravery, initiative, perseverance, and team spirit."

More applause.

Eddie looked out over the crowd, "Will the interns please step forward?"

The interns took a small step forward. The room was crowded and there wasn't much extra room to move forward anyway.

"Marcos, Lu Lu, Thebe, Andy, Liz, John, Dave, Paul…by the power vested in me by the Space Zoo Patrol Council, I hereby certify that you have successfully completed and graduated from the Space Zoo Patrol Intern Program, and that you are now fully accredited Space Zoo Patrol Junior Officers. Congratulations!"

The room was about to burst into applause, but Eddie held his paws up again and the room quieted down. "Also, let me read a personal message from the President of the Space Zoo Patrol Council, 'We have been watching your progress with great interest, and are very pleased with your accomplishments. If the Space Zoo Patrol finds one individual or one family here at home with a problem, we will then throw all our efforts into searching far and wide to help them. As we say, Think Locally…Act Galactically. Because of your efforts, the world is a better place. We look forward to your next contributions. We welcome you not just into the ranks of the Space Zoo Patrol officers but also into the arms of the Space Zoo Patrol family.' "

The room erupted into wild applause and those immediately behind the new graduates reached over to pat them on their backs.

"Wait, wait," said Eddie. "There is one more announcement. And this one is really official."

Everyone became silent.

He pushed a button on his computer and the big screen came on. Everyone looked over and saw a close up of Dr. Walstib. Walstib looked serious. Everyone on the bridge became serious.

"Greetings my Space Zoo Patrol friends. I'll make this brief. I am delighted with all of your amazing accomplishments. Thank you." He paused, then cleared his throat. "There is only one thing left to say…" He looked directly into the camera, gave a big smile, and said, "Party time!"

The music started and everyone sang and danced.

Marcos shouted to the other interns, "Hey. Where's the graduation cake?"

CHAPTER 73

SIX MONTHS LATER

Jim Slennar was smiling. He stood on a small ridge that overlooked thousands of acres of beautiful pink mushrooms. His team had created tons of their new sewage-food waste-yard waste quick-compost dirt and filled in the fields that had been empty for years due to soil erosion. The former Space Zoo Patrol interns, now junior officers, had brought down thousands of pink mushroom seeds and the seeds were growing well. Hundreds of small farmers harvested the crops and sold them to local markets. Now that Jim knew the system worked, he would duplicate the process around the world. Millions of people would have healthy, delicious, and inexpensive food. Of course, Slennar had help. He had hired four new interns, Glenn, Sally, Mario, and Kali.

Back up on Space Zoo 1, Eddie and Jane sat in their command chairs, as usual, and watched the world spin around.

"I've been thinking these last few months," said Jane. "And I've come up with the perfect way to solve our 'green-blue' versus 'blue-green' disagreement about the color of the hurricane research plane."

"I'm listening," said Eddie.

"I'd say the plane's color was aqua."

There was a long pause as they continued to look out the main windows.

"I like it," said Eddie.

They continued to watch the Earth.

After a while Eddie said, "Although, I'd say it was more of a turquoise."

ABOUT THE AUTHOR

Anthony G. Bennett received his BBA and MBA from The George Washington University. He has worked as a marketing professional for major corporations, as a White House appointee, as a registered lobbyist for the Solar Energy industry, as the editor of a marketing textbook, and has taught marketing as an adjunct lecturer for seven years at Georgetown University. He lives in McLean, VA and has twin boys.

Space Zoo Patrol

Made in the USA
Middletown, DE
16 May 2016